IN A DEEP BLUE HOUR

"In his finest novel yet, Stamm grapples with the riches and risks of a life lived at the mercy of one's art. As a character proclaims: 'Once you've read a book, you're never rid of it.' Dear reader, *In a Deep Blue Hour* is a book you won't want to be rid of, a book both birdhouse and bird, eggs in the head. A hatching, flapping achievement of the highest order."
—David James Poissant, author of *Lake Life* and
The Heaven of Animals

PRAISE FOR

PETER STAMM

"Stamm's prose (beautifully translated by Michael Hofmann) is plain but not so simple...A subtle but deadly style."
—Zadie Smith

"Peter Stamm is an extraordinary author who can make the ordinary absolutely electrifying...Hard to recommend too highly."
—Tim Parks

"A master writer...His prose...is as sharply illuminating as a surgical light."
—*The Economist*

these stories recall Arthur Schnitzler, or even Edgar Allan Poe...haunting...beautifully translated, as are all his books, by the remarkable Michael Hofmann." —*Harper's*

"[Stamm's] powerfully unsettling short-story collection catalogs moments when the familiar shifts into the unknown, when we realize how flimsy our constructed realties really are."
—*Literary Hub*, Most Anticipated Books of the Year

"From an author one critic called 'one of Europe's most exciting writers' come a dozen reflective and somber stories about the tenuousness of reality." —*Los Angeles Times*

"[These stories] all have a latent uneasiness to them, making the reader turn the pages both quickly and apprehensively...Stamm effectively sustains a dark mood."
—*Publishers Weekly*

"Stamm sketches out painfully realistic stories that slowly but surely reveal their strange, uneasy underbellies."
—*The Millions*, Most Anticipated Books

"Peter Stamm doesn't so much yank the rug out from under the reader as ease it slowly, mesmerizingly away, until we stagger and realize that the world has shifted beneath us. These tales are eerie, menacing delights."
—Caitlin Horrocks, author of *Life Among the Terranauts*

"A casual, effortless voice belies the intense structural formality in these stories, which take place on the blurred edge between reality, memory, and dream. Language is wielded subtly, sharply, in masterful hands. *It's Getting Dark* burns like ice."

—Shruti Swamy, author of *The Archer* and
A House Is a Body

THE SWEET INDIFFERENCE OF THE WORLD

"An entrancing tale about a writer haunted by his past self…[Stamm's] stripped-down, pared-back prose still works wonders, exploring complex issues and probing singular minds in a thoroughly compelling way."   —*Star Tribune*

"Acclaimed Swiss writer Peter Stamm tells the mysterious, complex story of a time-traveling love affair that tests the boundaries of reality and raises as many questions as it answers."   —*Vogue*, Best Books to Read This Winter

"Excellent…this amorphous tale folds in on itself, becoming a meditation on how memory can distort reality…Fans of Julian Barnes will love this."   —*Publishers Weekly*

"Haunting…The fascinating overall effect of *Indifference* makes it a worthy inclusion among Stamm's other compelling novels."   —*Literary Review*

"There's a satisfying tension between the complexity of the novel's conceit and the simplicity of the writing…lively and well paced, fully capturing the rhythm of two people walking and speaking...it's a novel about a writer and about people talking, which, in its distortions, takes on larger questions of storytelling and memory."   —*Los Angeles Review of Books*

"*The Sweet Indifference of the World* explores questions of time, identity, and art in prose that is dreamy, melancholic, and beautiful."   —*Book Riot*

"Adroitly translated by the award-winning Hofmann, [Stamm] explores the timeless doppelgänger phenomenon through dual couples whose fleeting interactions engender intriguing questions about singularity and agency and confirm the impossibility of absolutely sure answers."   —*Booklist*

"An elegant dart of a novel as clear and mesmerizing as an M. C. Escher drawing. I felt both lost and found at once. Peter Stamm is a truly wonderful writer."
    —Catherine Lacey, Whiting Award winner, Guggenheim fellow, and author of *Certain American States*, *The Answers*, and *Nobody Is Ever Missing*

IN A
DEEP
BLUE
HOUR

PETER
STAMM

*Translated from the German
by Michael Hofmann*

Other Press
New York

Copyright © 2023 Peter Stamm

Originally published in German as *In einer dunkelblauen Stunde* in 2023
by S. Fischer Verlag GmbH, Frankfurt am Main

Translation copyright © 2025 Michael Hofmann
We wish to express our appreciation to the Swiss Arts Council Pro Helvetia
for their assistance in the preparation of this translation.

swiss arts council
prohelvetia

Poetry extract on page 16 by Gottfried Benn, from the poem
"Blue Hour" in *Impromptus: Selected Poems and Some Prose*
(tr. Michael Hofmann, FSG, 2013), used by permission.

Verse on page 138 by Carl Sandburg.

Production editor: Yvonne E. Cárdenas
Text designer: Patrice Sheridan
This book was set in Simoncini Garamond and Agenda by
Alpha Design & Composition of Pittsfield, NH

10 9 8 7 6 5 4 3 2 1

Library of Congress Cataloging-in-Publication Data
Names: Stamm, Peter, 1963- author. | Hofmann, Michael, 1957
August 25- translator.
Title: In a deep blue hour : a novel / Peter Stamm ; translated from the
German by Michael Hofmann.
Other titles: In einer dunkelblauen Stunde. English
Description: New York : Other Press, 2025.
Identifiers: LCCN 2024030487 (print) | LCCN 2024030488 (ebook) |
ISBN 9781635424447 (paperback) | ISBN 9781635424454 (ebook)
Subjects: LCSH: Authors, Swiss—Fiction. | Motion picture producers and
directors—Fiction. | Documentary films—Fiction. | LCGFT: Novels.
Classification: LCC PT2681.T3234 I5313 2025 (print) |
LCC PT2681.T3234 (ebook) | DDC 833/.92—dc23/eng/20240709
LC record available at https://lccn.loc.gov/2024030487
LC ebook record available at https://lccn.loc.gov/2024030488

"I know not what tomorrow will bring…"

—FERNANDO PESSOA

IN A
DEEP
BLUE
HOUR

1

I DON'T KNOW
how much time I have left, says Wechsler, but then who
does? Sometimes I've felt closer to the end than I do
just now.

He is standing on the banks of the Seine, the sky is
overcast, a couple of pigeons fly past. Wechsler gesticulates,
as though to dispel the thought. In the background there's
a *bateau-mouche* going past at surprising speed. Wechsler
turns away from the camera, looks down at the river, shrugs.

What about starting with that?

That was after he told us about his accident in the
mountains, isn't that right? says Tom. He is sitting on the
bed, reading.

What's that you're reading? And it wasn't an accident,
just a near thing.

For Wechsler it was *un moment critique.*

Are you proposing that we take him up into the mountains and film him stumbling around remembering? If he
shows at all. We've heard the story anyway. Thomas.

Lately, he's wanted me to call him Thomas. Why would someone who for forty years has gone by Tom suddenly want to be Thomas? I rewind.

It would be nice if we could get some footage in the mountains, says Tom. Mountains always look good. Paris, the village, the mountains.

Presumably, the story gets more dramatic each time he tells it. What's that you're reading?

The hotel brochure. A brief voyage of discovery round the hotel, surrounded by varied scenery in idyllic wine-growing country. A sought-after gastronomic area, offering delights for every taste. An ideal venue for the combining of work and pleasure, free Internet connection, an El Dorado for the businessman.

What about the businesswoman?

There it is. I switch to play.

...got lost, says Wechsler, but instead of going back...you know I've always hated retracing my steps. I was going up an incline, steeper and steeper, and the footing was loose, I had the feeling nothing was moored anymore. And then I got to these boulders. I thought...I really had a sense of my own mortality...It suddenly struck me...

He has the annoying quality of not finishing his sentences. You know what he means, but he never says it. We can't make a film of all broken-off sentences.

I push fast-forward.

...but then who does, says Wechsler. Sometimes I've felt closer to the end than I do just now.

We could stick it at the end, says Tom. As a perspective. The film's over, life goes on. And he walks into the sunset, at that little lake. There's one of his books that ends like that.

No, that was the sea, I say. I'd like to have my own room.

I'm going for a walk, says Tom. Thomas.

Thomas? I can't keep a straight face when I call him that.

Andrea? he says, and looks at me expectantly. He climbs down off the bed with a groan and puts on his shoes.

Why don't your shoes have laces? And why haven't I noticed that before?

They're Japanese.

And the Japanese can't tie shoelaces? Bah! I ought to go out myself. I'm going stir-crazy in here.

TOM WAS gone all afternoon. I would have liked to go for a walk myself, but we're not here for fun, we only have so many days we can film on. Paris was a strain on the budget as it was, with the hotel and meals. Even if there's not much we can do just at the moment, I think it's important to be here, keep some sort of presence. That's a typical Wechsler word: presence. He was supposed to arrive today, and I went to the station to collect him but he wasn't on the train he said he would be on. Perhaps he got the day wrong.

Call him, Tom said.

He doesn't have a mobile.

Of course he has a mobile, I've seen him with it.

Well, then he hasn't shared the number. I'll send him an email.

I sent him one already. That was this morning, and he hasn't replied. I've eaten nothing all day.

I take a sheet of paper, and write: Childhood, Mountains, Water, Paris, Women. And then one more: Books. Who is the woman? I write. I crumple up the paper and throw it in the bin.

I play around with our footage, piece together a short video. Wechsler walking. He crosses Montparnasse Cemetery, he walks along a broad boulevard, he walks in the Luxembourg Gardens. He walks down a different boulevard, he strolls along the banks of the Seine, looking at the secondhand book stalls, he takes a book out of one of the boxes, a book of photographs, flicks through it, takes it and pays. He walks down a narrow lane, the camera is close behind him. He approaches the camera, he does something with his hand in front of his face, it looks nice. Even though he has this unworldly demeanor, he has a pretty good idea of what looks good on film. He walks past the camera. I could make a two-hour film of Wechsler walking in Paris. He enters a bakery, comes out again, says something, and laughs. That was when he bought croissants for all of us. He can be charming sometimes.

Something has got my attention, but I couldn't say what it is. Something somehow out of the ordinary. I play through the video again. Now I notice the same woman in the background of two of the sequences, first in the cemetery, then on the boulevard. She's too far away, and I can't really see her features, but she's wearing a light-green raincoat, which is fairly unusual. Also her movements seem the same, there's something skippy about her walk, I'm sure it's the same woman. Maybe it's coincidence, but they were shot at different times. Curious. Another Wechsler word, that: curious.

Now I wonder what's keeping Tom?

SOMETHING HAPPENED that day, I don't know what, but it wasn't anything good. It was the last day of the shoot in Paris, we had met up as always in the café on the Rue du Bac, the Café Les Mouettes. I don't know of anywhere in the world that you would associate less with seagulls. Maybe there's somewhere in the Gobi Desert, or the South Pole. To begin with, we'd assumed it was Wechsler's local, then it turned out that he had picked it at random and had never been there. I think he wanted to meet us in a neutral place. Or maybe lay a false trail. It could easily be my local, he said, if I had anything like that.

At our first meeting in the Café Les Mouettes, he pointed out a little gate that led to a courtyard and then to the Chapelle de l'Epiphanie of the Missions Etrangères. From here thousands of missionaries were dispatched all over the world, to make converts...He spotted the Nespresso store next door, and laughed. These are the missionaries of today. Coffee for all, the new epiphany of taste.

Toward the end of the filming that day, I noticed that Wechsler was in a bad mood, and something was annoying him. Early afternoon, postlunch slump, typical. There was a bit of trouble with the microphone, Wechsler was impatient, though he sought to disguise it. He always tries to keep everything under wraps. It was Tom who was conducting the interview this time.

The unnamed narrator in your books, that's always you, isn't it?

I'd gone on and on to him about never asking that question, so presumably it was the first thing that leapt into his mind, maybe the only thing he could remember.

It's not, Wechsler replies, it's you, Tom, didn't you notice?

Tom's expression made me laugh. Luckily you can't hear it on the soundtrack. Wechsler grinned.

Let's talk about women, then, says Tom from out of shot. They are very important in your writing, but you've never been married.

Wechsler's expression goes rigid, he stares straight into the camera. For a moment I wonder if he's even heard the question, or was off in his thoughts somewhere. Then, very slowly and in a pained voice, as though explaining something to a clueless child, What else am I going to write about? Keeping rabbits? Tom laughs awkwardly. The evening before, he had laid out his theory about Wechsler and women, a complicated structure of desire and seduction, with narcissism and Wechsler's mother also involved, or maybe it was his father, I'm no longer sure. He had another theory, too, about confrontational communication, which he was evidently just putting to the test. For now he seems to have come up short anyway, because a long silence ensues.

Is it more important to you to love or to be loved? he finally asks. I mean, honestly, what a question.

What a question! says Wechsler. Is this a film about books or bed? I write about men and women because men and women populate our world. He gets up, and I take off after him with the camera. He stalks out of the café.

The camera stays fixed on the door for a moment, then pans to the side, you see Wechsler outside the café, lighting a cigarette, people go by, a flash of green, it's not the woman in the raincoat again, is it? Traffic, a bus, a bicycle messenger in a hi-vis jacket. You hear the noise of cars on the soundtrack, and Wechsler's voice, softly, he's still miked up. I play through the footage a couple of times before I can make out what he's saying: This isn't going anywhere. Afterward, he apologized for his behavior.

That was the day I first wondered why Wechsler was even participating in our project, as he wanted not to give anything of himself away. Even in one of our preliminary conversations he quoted Pessoa: If after my life you want to write my biography, nothing simpler. It consists of two dates—birth and death. All the days between are mine. What did he think we were going to make a film about?

At six, Tom reappears. He walks in without knocking, but I don't feel like training him anymore; all that's over.

I found the butcher, he says.

Now it's my turn to go out for a bit. I'd like some fresh air too.

In the doorway, I turn to look at him. Well, and is it more important to love or to be loved?

He gives me his most gormless expression.

I DON'T understand this place. I continually lose my way in it, even though the center isn't even very big. I keep losing my way, and don't know where I am. I could have sworn there was a supermarket across the street in front of the hotel, but there's a large, mostly empty parking lot.

It's all honeycombed with passages, lanes, alleyways, in which you can lose your way. I made note of a couple of places that Wechsler mentioned in conversation: the school, the church, the bar he met his friends at, also the address of his parents on the other side of the railway tracks. I wonder what it would feel like to know all these places, these streets and buildings, the people there, a network of stories and memories. For me, it's just a place like any other, neither big nor small, neither strikingly beautiful nor particularly ugly.

As I get to the station, a freight train is just passing through. I compulsively count the cars, the way I always did when I was a girl. Thirteen. Didn't they use to be longer? Or does it just seem like that to me, because

I'm bigger, so they seem shorter? Because I'm better at counting?

I walk through the underpass and come to a precinct with single-family homes. It's remarkably cold for the time of year, and I wish I'd brought a sweater.

There's nothing arresting here. The houses all seem to come from the forties and fifties, a few are new. The gardens are well tended. There are children playing on the street. I wonder what it was like here forty or fifty years ago? Presumably not much different. Only the carports and garages, which clearly every house needs, seem new. This is where Wechsler will have played on the street, back in the day, and ridden around on his bicycle, and perched on the garden fence and chatted with the kids next door. I wonder if everything was already present in him then? The dim foreknowledge of pain? What will these children one day become? Carpenters, teachers, accountants, writers? Suddenly, they're all grown-up, and nothing is the way it used to be.

You need a village, Wechsler said in the course of one of our conversations, not to be alone anymore. The people and the plants and the soil all harbor a bit of you, and even if you don't know it, it's there waiting for you. A couple of sentences he managed to finish, and not before time. But then he wasn't their author. So who was it? And is it even true? Is there anything left of Wechsler hereabouts? Isn't it that a bit of here will have survived in him?

Eighteen, twenty, twenty-two, the next one must be the house he grew up in. A middle-aged woman is standing by the garden gate, seeming like she might be waiting for someone. His sister, maybe, or his sister-in-law? Does he even have siblings? No idea. Does it matter?

I wonder about speaking to the woman, but before I reach her, she's turned around and gone back into the house, as though she wanted to hide from me. The name on the mailbox doesn't mean anything to me.

I DON'T know if we wanted to help Wechsler or help ourselves, and what his motives were and ours. Maybe all that doesn't matter. You have to do something to pass the time. One reason harbors many reasons—who was it said that? None of the three of us had exactly achieved a lot in the last few years, he had a book of prose miniatures that had all been published before, and we had a few unrealized film projects that we had managed to get grants for that just about kept the wolf from the door, and one or two little films for museums. That was when we ran into Wechsler. Authors comment on items in the collection. He had selected an Edward Hopper painting, no, my mistake, it was a Felix Vallotton. Whatever made me think it was Hopper?

The artist is like a lover, touching the model or the landscape and touched by them. The painting is an act of love, a celebration of beauty. That kind of thing. There are artists who almost recede behind their art: Vallotton is more present in his paintings than most. And yet we don't know much about him.

And what do we know about Richard Wechsler? Astonishingly little, if you think we're making a film about him. The article in Wiki, a couple of newspaper interviews. We attended a reading he gave, and we've read his books, at least the greater part of them. You don't need much to make a film. Some pretty pictures.

I had another look at the museum film when I got back to the hotel. Wechsler reads from a prepared script, it sounds awfully wooden. I wonder if he's even present in his works. And how? The lover of his characters? That sounds a bit sketchy, doesn't it? Pathetic? Pornographic? Warped?

Great art leaves traces of itself in us, says Wechsler; even when the words and pictures pale or mutate in us, their effect endures. Their scarring. Strange word to use. What effect do his books have on me? Is he answerable for it? Is that all deliberate, or am I just a chance victim? What's the expression again? Is my response just collateral damage? All I know is that the effect on me of him as a person was like that of his books, but maybe that was more to do with me than him. It felt as though something was at one and the same time quite right and totally wrong. Tom had been an admirer for a long time, he had read everything of Wechsler's and passed it on to me. I had only read two or three of the books, but then as preparation for the film, I of course read all the others as well, or most of them at any rate. I wonder whether they had the same effect on Tom as they did on me? I somehow doubt it. When we talked about them, it was as though we had been reading different books.

Whose idea was the film? I think it was Tom who first raised it as a possibility, but it was Wechsler who had got

him, or got us, to the point where the thing just had to
be said and we'd known it all along. I wanted to see him
again, that was undeniably the case. Because I had to find
out what it was with the wrong right or the right wrong.
Just because his treatment of us was so casual. Polite, but
casual. He was never really there in the museum. Never
present. If he'd courted us, built himself up in front of us,
I am sure I would have lost interest in him like that, and
the thing would be dead, but instead I had the impression
that it was of no importance to him whatsoever, that he
couldn't have been less interested. After the shoot I felt a
kind of emptiness. He sucks me dry, was one of the first
impressions I noted down about him. He's a vampire, living off the blood of others. Such nonsense.

When in fact it was Wechsler who once referred to us
as cannibals. You live off the heart's blood of the people
you consume, he said, a most equivocal profession. That's
why it's so important that you conduct it with love and
honesty, yes, with honesty but also with tact. That's what
you owe me.

Tom doesn't think about such matters. He's basically
a simple soul. Friendly enough, he wouldn't hurt a fly, but
simple. If every man were like that, the world would be a
different place, no doubt better, but also duller. I used to
call him Tomcat early on, and he liked that well enough,
though he was more like a dog really. A loyal companion
who will stand for any sort of treatment. Eventually he
was just a pain. And now he wants to be Thomas, which
only makes the whole thing even sadder. Rex the Runt, I

remember those cartoons with the abject dog. That's what I ought to call Tom instead.

The way he behaved during the shoot was embarrassing. It was all Mr. Wechsler this, Mr. Wechsler that. Does the microphone bother you? Can I bring you a glass of water? I was just waiting for him to stretch out on his back and let him scratch his tummy for him. My own relationship with Wechsler was different from the start, it was a test of strength. Had he been ten years younger, I'm sure he would have tried to flirt with me, now he just hinted at it, complimented me, told me I reminded him of someone.

A woman you liked?

Another question he left unanswered. Maybe that's why I can't let go of him: because he owes me so many answers. So what feelings do I have for him? He bugs me, but not the way Tom does. What's the expression again? He gives me an inch... No, that's not apt here.

DO YOU want to use that, then? asks Tom.

He came up behind me while I was looking at the museum film again. I don't like it when people look over my shoulder. It doesn't mean I'm hiding anything, I just don't like it.

Of course not, I was just playing it back to myself. It might give me an idea.

The film's in a completely different idiom.

I know that.

He puts his hand on my shoulder. I get up to open the window. It's begun raining, the rain sounds a little like distant applause. I feel like buying myself a pair of jeans or a T-shirt, some underwear. I could use a belt. But the shops are shut now.

You always get the best conversations when the camera's not running. One time, when we'd been filming on the banks of the Seine, Tom and Sascha, who was doing the sound for us in Paris, were packing up. Wechsler and I smoked a cigarette, I was still smoking at the time. A flock of pigeons flew just over our heads, it felt like an air attack that they'd aborted at the last moment.

We were talking about the point and the pointlessness of these kind of film portraits. What's next is as I remember it: I thought, Wechsler was saying, I thought I would learn something about myself from your way of looking at me. But that's nonsense. How can a person who doesn't know me from Adam discover anything about me that I haven't known long since? You show exactly what I am able to show of myself, not more, not less. Or probably less, at that. And a day later, it'll be different.

I said I did indeed have aspirations to capture the person I was portraying, and to say something truthful about them. So you're giving yourself an hour to capture the truth about a human being? he said. That's something I haven't managed in my entire life.

A film isn't the work of just an hour.

He smiles.

There's something blue in him, I can't think of another way of putting it. He is smooth and gleaming and diaphanous, sometimes he's as solid seeming as glass, sometimes more like a drop of water that would run away if you touched it. The blue part of him isn't much. If he's careless, you can see it in his eyes. But when he's reserved, his eyes are like reflecting mirrors, showing me nothing but myself. It's the blue part that his stories come from, not all of them, but the best ones. It's not possible to muddy that blue. True blue. If only I were able to show that. Wasn't there a film once that was all blue? For an hour or more, a blue screen. Right, that was Derek Jarman, who was almost blind at the time from HIV/AIDS. In fact, it's mostly just a sound reel with diary entries, memories, bits of philosophizing, items on politics and aesthetics, spiritual guff, and some esoteric music played over it, the whole thing pretentious and self-pitying and, worst of all, boring. Is it all right to say that when someone's dying? It is. But I thought the idea of it was fantastic, a film without images. You close your eyes, and fall into space.

Music without notes, that was 4'33", by John Cage. A picture that consists of a frame, a hole in the screen, James Turrell's Skyspaces. What about a book without words, has anyone ever done that? Is it even possible?

I kept the hotel window open the whole time in Paris. Tom complained about it, but I liked the street noise that kept going till late at night, the swelling and abating waves of it, the changing tones of cars and trucks, delivery trucks and motorbikes. Sometimes it completely stops for moments at a time, but then it starts again. There's a horn tooting, not aggressively, more like an appeal, a squealing brake, voices, laughter. I am standing naked in the hotel window, the city is being born out of me. A siren comes closer, moves away again. Any one of those sirens would have a more exciting story to tell than all my books put together, says Wechsler. There are plane trees in front of the hotel, and I can see the river between the leaves.

My red suitcase is on the bed. I pack up my things, walk around. Wechsler watches me, smiles, fiddles with a ballpoint pen, takes a sip of water, clears his throat. Yes? Is there something he wants to say? What is he even doing here? I put on clean clothes, bundle up the dirty things, get my toiletry bag from the bathroom, books, all the paper printouts that you have in any production, a couple of external hard drives, one or two things I've bought myself, a scent, L'Heure Bleue by Guerlain. I never use scent, I only bought it for the name. *In a blue, a deep blue hour, and when it's gone no one knows if it was.*

WECHSLER PUTS out his cigarette, walks over to the nearest bin. I trot along after him, throw away my stub as well. I feel like going for a drink with him. He seems to be pondering, hesitates.

Tom and Sascha have finally finished packing up, and are heading in our direction, they're maybe a hundred yards away. Wechsler is suddenly shy, unsure, the blue is very clearly there now, then it vanishes. Let's go, he says quickly. And we do, we run off together. Tom calls out after us, but with the tripod and the heavy bag of equipment, he's much slower than we are. I don't even bother to turn around. I just trot off with Wechsler and laugh out loud in relief.

I am in a state of exhilaration because I have left Tom and Sascha behind. I know I've behaved badly and for no reason, and that just makes me merrier. I feel the way I did when I cut class, like an adventuress. And Wechsler is my accomplice.

We're sitting at a café on one of the islands in the Seine, we haven't gone far, I am drinking a glass of white wine, a Pouilly-Fumé that Wechsler recommended. There's a whole long story about this particular wine, which he tells me, but it's not relevant now. Sometimes he just talks a streak, without it being about anything, and then he suddenly loses interest in the subject and stops.

Wechsler is drinking a Ricard, and there's a story about that too. How he used to not like Ricard, and then started drinking it anyway. There's a story to everything, it's like one of those Mandelbrot fractals where each pattern contains further, finer patterns, you can go up to it as close as you like and you'll never get to the end, a story within a story within a story.

Most of the other people in the café seem to be tourists, they are drinking beer, but it all looks deeply authentic just the same. This idyllic square beside the river with the two trees, and are they lime trees? The terrace, the little tables, and the woven chairs. The waiter with his brisk politeness, even the pigeons, though you get them everywhere. But this is where they fit in best. The city just lets us get on with it, there's something so liberating about that.

Did I tell you this is my first time in Paris?

Well? he asks, as if he cared.

It looks just exactly like what I imagined. It's as though I knew it all already.

The city's not like this all over.

Later on, Wechsler says: I always went away. That was my way out of any difficult or unpleasant situation. Leave. As long as you stay on the move, not much can happen to you.

But you've been living here for thirty years, I say, for thirty-three years, in fact. Isn't that right?

He doesn't answer.

Later: I was never able to believe that a woman truly loved me. That I was worth her love.

Would he say that? To someone he hardly knew? Or maybe *only* to someone he hardly knew? Is it a tactic? Is he flirting with me? I'm sure he has better technique than that. Then you don't just walk in with a crash.

That's sad.

Not really, he says, there's something liberating about it too. Fear is the possibility of freedom.

What fear do you mean?

The fear of loneliness.

You would never say that to me on camera.

Of course not. He laughs. I'm not stupid.

If I were making a feature film based on your life, then I could put in all those things. All the things you say off the record, the things I sense but couldn't prove. The true blue.

Am I on trial here?

No one's accusing you of anything if you're not.

Not even that, he says with a sad smile.

Thomas has a theory about your relationships with women.

I'm sure he does, says Wechsler. But you don't believe any of that nonsense, do you? Women. What women? Do they even exist, women? Anyway, films don't exist to carry theories.

What are they for then?

Silence is much more effective than spouting some kind of nonsense.

WILL YOU find your way back?

This would be the moment, but he doesn't take the opportunity. Presumably, the situation is too complicated for him. Does he know that I'm with Tom? That we're in a crisis? I'm sure he sensed it. Would the film be in danger if he...if we...Maybe I'm not his type. Does he like girls in jeans and fleece? Does he like short hair? Wide hips and small breasts? Does he like women who look like dog owners? And what about me? What do I think? Do I like him? Or would he be just a conquest? Does it matter?

The hotel's on the river, I can hardly get lost.

Upstream or down?

That way.

I need to go this way. He points to the opposite bank. See you tomorrow.

But then he doesn't leave the spot. I light a cigarette and wait for him to go. He seems uncertain again, probably waiting for me to go first. Another one of our trials of strength.

It was established in our very first discussion that he won't let us film in his house. He's even kept us from finding out his address: he preferred that we communicate via email. When I offered to send him some of our earlier films, he said I was to bring them to our next meeting. Our agreement, et cetera, all to be dealt with by his publisher. We're both standing outside the café like a couple of extras waiting for their cue. Tom's bound to be wondering what's keeping me. I look at my watch.

All right, then...he says, and gestures jerkily, as though wiping something away, and he heads off. After a few steps he has to stop at a light. He turns to look. I'm still standing there, I wave to him, smile. One–nothing to me. Now he crosses the street, even though the lights are still red, he's taking his life in his hands, a car honks at him. I get the sense he's running away from me.

I give him a head start, then set off in pursuit. He crosses the bridge, and keeps going along the riverbank, not an especially cozy area, a multilane highway, slightly rundown apartment blocks, seventies presumably, a few trees.

I imagine the two of us as the same age. No, he's younger than me. He's just had his first novel published. *On the Edge of Sleep*. What's my role? Never mind. No, I need a role, let's keep this realistic. I've come to Paris to make a short documentary profile about him. Just a couple of minutes for a culture program, local cameraman, a one-day shoot.

Or better: I'm doing it for the radio. No cameraman, no pictures, just the two of us and a recorder. What was the technology they were using at the time? MiniDisc or DAT? I'm the experienced culture editor, he's the inexperienced first-time author. We've met at a café, but there was too much noise, the espresso machine, the jingle of cups and glasses, the conversations going on all around us.

We could go back to my hotel room, it's quiet there. I laugh.

A little chancy. On the other hand, could be perfectly innocent. We're grown-up. But he's hungry, and so am I.

Okay.

The hotel is nearby, we walk there silently, he's always a step or two behind me. I'm dragging him along, so to speak.

Do they allow gentlemen callers here? he asks, as we pass reception to the elevator. Cheeky! I don't respond.

Upstairs, I go into the bathroom to freshen up, open another button on my blouse, look in the mirror, do it up again.

When I step back into the room, he's standing by the window, silently looking out. He has a cute butt. There's only one chair in the room. I push it over nearer the bed. Sit down. I sit on the bed, put on the earphones. One, two, three. Can you say something for levels? What did you have for breakfast? Our knees are touching.

THE NEIGHBORHOOD, if anything, seems to be getting worse, the expressway is now four lanes wide and is being fed on a descending ramp under a bridge. We are on a bike path between the river and the road. Just as well Wechsler doesn't turn around. Not surprisingly, there're no other pedestrians anywhere, and nowhere to hide. I let myself fall back a little farther. After the bridge we return to ground level, up another ramp, and Wechsler turns into a side street with a large building at the end of it. That must be the station we arrived at, I recognize the clock tower.

Wechsler enters the station at a side entrance on the lower level. I run for a few steps and have to jump over a large puddle; once I'm in the station, I can't see him anywhere. To the left are the Intercité trains, the ones to the right are suburban lines. Suddenly I'm standing in a large, low-ceilinged departure hall crowded with people, and with lots of platforms off to both sides, intersections, arrows pointing to various Métro lines and the RER. Wechsler is gone, vanished.

I then walked up into the main departure hall, got myself a coffee, and read the destinations on the next trains, Marseilles, Nice, Grenoble, Toulon, I want to play for time.

At the barrier, a young couple is saying goodbye. They kiss, the man is carrying an enormous bag, which he gives the woman, who carries it through the barrier. Once on the other side, she turns around and kisses her hand at him, which looks a bit foolish and theatrical to me. I wonder, did I ever kiss my hand at anyone? In earnest, at least?

The man is about my age, perhaps a shade younger. He looks up at me as we pass each other. Did he notice me watching him and his girlfriend? Or perhaps they're married.

I follow him out of the station, this time I'm less cautious and walk close behind him, he doesn't know me, and I've got nothing to lose.

I'M THINKING of growing my hair long. All young women these days seem to have long hair. Why wouldn't I?

What did you have for breakfast?

Nothing.

Our knees touch. He lowers his eyes, looks down at my knees, puts his hand on them, and pushes my skirt up. I am unusually passive in this situation, don't know what to do with my microphone or the recorder, what to do with my hands. We should stand up, then I'd have more flexibility. We stand up, hug, kiss. He is a few inches taller than me. Now he drops to his knees to lift my skirt off. I can feel he is aroused. I am as well.

After the young man has walked a little way down the boulevard, he takes a seat at one of the small tables outside a café. I sit a couple of tables away, and he doesn't notice me until the waiter comes to take our orders. I have what he's having, *la même chose que monsieur*. In the young man's eyes I can see him thinking: Where has he seen me before? Then he remembers and smiles.

That night I was late getting back to the hotel. Tom made a stink. What did I think I was playing at? We were a team, after all. He really is in a temper, inasmuch as he ever can be. I almost like him again. I open the window, and the night comes in. I stand by the window, like a conductor in front of the orchestra of the city. Tom is still griping. I turn around and kiss him on the mouth. Don't worry about it. I have a shower, afterward we sleep together. We haven't done that for a while.

In the morning, before everything gets going, that's what Wechsler said that night in the café, the fresh air, the level sunbeams. When everything begins afresh, when it gets going, when it resumes. A quote, inevitably, lifted from someone or other. He told me who, but I didn't know the name and forgot it again right away. I've never gotten into the habit of waking beside anyone, he said to me. Any relationships I've had were more or less against my own will. They were good for me, and but for them I wouldn't have survived as long as I have. But I've never been able to endure proximity to anyone else for any length of time, I would have made a good sea captain, back in the day, someone who comes and goes with the same enthusiasm.

Later on: If I'd been given the choice, I would probably have stayed alone, not done anything, just contemplated the world.

But you do have the choice.

Just to sit in a café and watch people, the traffic going by, the buses and cars, the bikes, the motorbikes. And above all, the birds. And then write all of it down. The attempt to capture the totality of a place, nothing more than that.

Why the birds?

I don't know. Peculiar, that's the word that springs to mind for me. It's all very peculiar. *Étrange.* Strange. Not do anything, just wait and watch as the time goes by, and write it all down, commit it to paper. In the morning.

THE BUTCHER. It was Tom who found him, he was so pleased with himself. There's a good boy, do you want a cookie? The butcher is a childhood friend of Wechsler's, they went to school together. We meet him the next day. Wechsler still hasn't showed up, so we decided to talk to a few people who knew him. Strictly speaking, it's against our agreement, but then he's in breach of it himself. We don't have to use their material. At any rate, it's better to go out and film something than sit around the gloomy hotel room all day and not know what to do with ourselves.

The butcher. He was on our radar because Wechsler wrote a column about him once. About sausage-making. That he could see himself spending a whole day talking to an old friend who now makes sausages, because sausage-making is as much an art as writing books. He went on to belabor the metaphor some more. Is it even an art? Not really. But then there are times you need to say something, you're under pressure, even if it's not quite up to snuff. Wechsler laughed. Anyway, yesterday afternoon Tom went to all the butchers in the whole place, there weren't that many of them, truth be told there were two, and he established which of them went to school with Wechsler. He has a small butcher's shop on the other side of the tracks.

So you went to school with Richard Wechsler?

Even as we're miking him up in his white tunic, I know he's not going to help us a bit. Chatting to Tom when there's no one else in the store is different. But now he's standing outside his butcher's shop with a mike under his nose and a camera in his face. He says hello to every single passerby. They make foolish remarks to him, Hey, are you going to be on TV then? Are you in trouble? Did your bratwursts win a medal or something? His shy smile, his professional smile. Of course he's embarrassed, but they're his customers.

Seems to always happen—during the sound check they go silent. They chatter away all day long, but the minute they're required to say something to order, they clam up. I ask the old standby question: What did you have for breakfast? To which Wechsler says: Nothing. And is silent again. The butcher at least broke his fast.

Afterward, I look at the recording in slow motion. The rapid sequence of emotions in his face was fascinating to observe, his features shifting about like little gusts of wind. Confusion, astonishment, awkwardness, an honest attempt to call something to mind, and then sealed features, almost resistance, I'm damned if I tell them.

And in fact he really didn't tell us much. Only one thing: he did go to school with Wechsler. Wechsler was a good student, a clown, but shy as well. He was either the focus of attention or else he was all alone, he was never a fellow traveler. They used to play table tennis together. None of the others knew much about him really. Then the butcher uses a surprising term. He says: Wechsler was very painstaking. In everything. Tom doesn't ask a follow-up, he never does, you can tell he's a cameraman, not a journalist.

Has he read any of Wechsler's books? The butcher laughs and shakes his head. I'm not much of a reader.

The butcher speaks. He was once in Paris with Wechsler and another male and a female friend—three men and a woman. At the time, they were all still living in the village, but Wechsler had some sort of connection to Paris, the butcher isn't quite clear what it was. Maybe he really doesn't remember. Or could it be that Wechsler was already living there then? In that case, they certainly wouldn't have taken a hotel room. They went to a restaurant that served these big twenty-ounce steaks.

They were a bit much even for me, says the butcher, laughing. But it was good meat. The French do certain cuts differently than we do.

Was the woman with Wechsler then? asks Tom. He insisted on conducting the interview himself, after all it was he who had tracked down the butcher. I'm doing the camera, which is usually his job, only we've always had the odd exception. He's good with simple people. It's because I'm one of them—he's said it so often now that no one believes him any longer. Anyway, what does that mean, simple people? The butcher's certainly not simple, I could tell that right away. We were just friends, he says, old school friends. Why should he tell us anything? What good would it do him? I could tell from his eyes that he's keeping things back. He laughs.

What he's not telling us is this: They took two double rooms. They drew lots for who was sharing with whom. Wechsler was with the woman in one room. The woman said to him: Whatever happens, we'll stay friends. The next day, in a museum, the butcher caught Wechsler and the woman kissing. They had lost the other two, the butcher went back to find the toilet, and he turned a corner and saw them in a passionate clinch. He turned on his heels and pretended not to have seen anything. But Wechsler had seen him. The butcher doesn't say so. And how do I know? The scene appears in one of Wechsler's books. Did it happen like that? Not certain, but it's a nice scene to picture.

We were just friends, says the butcher. He laughs nervously, greets a woman passing by, unclips his microphone.

WHAT'S TO prove the woman is the one in all his books? His first love?

Tom asked the butcher for the names of the other two who went to Paris with them, at least he managed that. The butcher just laughed again and said it was so long ago. The girl was the minister's daughter, he said, and laughed again, but it wasn't a dirty laugh, more a laugh of surprise. Judith, her name is. It would be, that's a kind of minister's daughter's name. In Wechsler's story, the woman is called something else. And the butcher isn't a butcher either. And the central figure isn't Wechsler.

At noon, it started raining again. If it didn't rain, we'd have a different film—strange thought. It's not about the village or this particular day, much less the weather, and yet I'm convinced that the film would have taken a different turn if the sun had been shining.

So we stayed in the hotel. Tom is sitting on the bed again, I'm in the chair by the window. I'm scouting around on the Internet, and I find a list of all the ministers who have officiated here since the Middle Ages. It really does start in the sixteenth century—impressive, no? One man officiated here between 1968 to 1981, he must be the girl's father. I google him, find a couple of entries, nothing terribly interesting, minister here, minister there, member of some commission or other, Google Books has a snippet of something on a Historical Association for Lake Constance in 1976, which is just a list of names and places...Dr. Müller from Tägerwilen, Herr Rutishauser from Steckborn, Herr Gemperli from Diessenhofen, Dr. Good from Hüttlingen, Dr. Dantz from Hörhausen, the Reverend Imbach...Finally, a eulogy that finishes with a quotation from the minister himself, unsourced. His last words, perhaps? A letter, to be opened in the event of his passing? This all was part of my life: was offered to me, was permitted me to give and to experience. I write these lines in a spirit of gratitude to the One who gave me so much, and thinking back with gratitude on the people I met on my path.

It reminds me of something, but I'm not sure what. A man drawing up his final accounts when face to face with death. Then it comes back to me: the diary of the polar explorer Robert Falcon Scott, his last entries on the way back from the South Pole, when he knows they're not going to make it alive: outside the door of the tent, it remains a scene of whirling drift. We shall stick it out to the end, but we are getting weaker, of course, and the end cannot be far. It seems a pity, but I do not think I can write more. For God's sake look after our people!

The minister has nothing to do with our film or with Wechsler. I am wasting my time. At least I've got the girl's Christian name and surname. Unless she got married in the meantime. In those days, women would routinely take their husband's name, I always thought that was weird. If she's done that it would be hard to track her down.

I hunt up the name, a handful of results. One Judith Imbach won a hundred-franc shopping voucher as a prize in a sudoku contest. Another woman of that name is mentioned in the supplement to the general encyclopedia of the Swiss confederation and its allied territories, edited by Johann Jakob Holzhalb, published in 1795. She appears in a long list of Uttinger or Uttiger family members, Francis Johann Jakob, eldest son, b. 1712, chaplain of the old church of Cham, m. Judith Maria Imbach, 6 daughters, 4 sons, of whom 3 died in infancy. Another Judith Imbach died seven years ago, aged ninety-two, it can't have been her either. She has been called by the Almighty, who holds our life in His hands, into the new life of the Hereafter. Her love and care were for her family. The Catholic ceremony took place in the church at Inwil, not even the religion is right.

I google Inwil. It's a village I've never been to, in Central Switzerland. In the last fifty years, the number of inhabitants has risen by a factor of ten. A local expressed unhappiness about the fact, and said he could remember when there were just four hundred inhabitants, and everyone knew exactly who had a toothache or a tummy upset.

What if Wechsler had been born there? A different life, a different person. Maybe he would have become an accountant or a priest or a policeman.

What are you doing? Tom asks from bed.

He's reading a book of Wechsler's, *All the Days of My Life*, appeared five years ago, the last proper book he published. Not that there was a lot of usable stuff in it either. It's always the same scenes in all the books, the same locations, the village of his childhood, Paris, then a bunch of unnamed others, provincial holes, sprawl, industrial landscapes and water, rivers, lakes, ponds. And very often that one woman, the love of his youth, who seems to have obsessed him. It's a bit of a surprise that anyone reads the stuff at all.

Looking at death announcements.

Tom raises his eyebrows, but doesn't say anything. He's put away the book and opened up his laptop.

I've closed the page of death notices and have started googling a few of my old beaux. Who would have guessed. One turns up on the website of a golf club. My word, he's put on weight. Another one is involved in alternative medicine, one of those therapies that I can't tell apart with names like tae kwon do or something. He looks reasonably well-preserved, but he was so insanely jealous I had to give him the boot. I check up on the Paris weather. Fourteen centigrade, scattered showers.

Did you know there were over six hundred types of pasta worldwide? Tom asks me.

He starts listing them: spaghetti, cannelloni, pappardelle, fusilli, orecchiette. He counts them on his fingers like a kid. Rice noodles, glass noodles, udon noodles. That was about it for him.

If you get to thirty, I'll buy you an ice cream.

I look up the weather in Moscow, in New York, in LA, in Buenos Aires, in Ouagadougou, even though I've not got the foggiest idea where that is.

A couple of Swedes—no, it was a Swede and a Franco-German—made a film together about people diving off a ten-meter board for the first time. Why didn't we think of that. They just show the board. And the people jumping off it. Or not. I'll send you the link.

The weather in Kuala Lumpur, in Tokyo, in Sydney. The weather at the South Pole. The daytime temperature sometimes touches minus fifty-eight centigrade. At night, it's always under minus sixty. Chance of precipitation: zero. Sunshine: zero.

Tom says he's going out to get some footage of the village, atmospherics, the market, the school, old people, youngsters, a cat in the rain.

Birds, I call out after him. Get some shots of birds. Wechsler loves birds.

THOSE SWEDES. I found an interview with them. Entirely forgettable names, especially the one that's not a Swede at all, he's French or Belgian. Axel, who's the bona fide Swede, says: I'd had enough of forcing reality into certain shapes, I was looking for a form where the image is sufficient. He says: I have no interest in making another film in which I end up telling lies about life. Protagonist, antagonist, conflict, story, moral. Everything follows that scheme.

Is that what we're doing then? Protagonist: Wechsler. Antagonist: The mystery woman? Or time passing? And the conflict? Death? The story? The moral? Is that the solution: Showing people jumping off a ten-meter board? Or not jumping?

But I can understand those Swedes, or that Swede and his Belgian chum. I know that feeling. There are too many stories everywhere, and all structured the same: plot point one, plot point two, resolution. Every damned car advertisement tells a story now. Paradise: the place without stories.

Emails, emails, emails, one from the producer, one from Sascha, the sound woman. The landlord. Now what does he want? Shock ventilation? What's that supposed to be. Sometimes I just don't have the strength to answer all the emails. But the fewer I answer, the more they get to be, and I end up without the strength to answer a single one of them. Does the fewer exist in an intensified form? The even fewer? But counting up varieties of pasta. I'm not there yet.

FINDING THE woman turns out to be dead easy. She is living in the village, is married, as I thought, but has kept her maiden name. She has followed her father into the ministry.

I couldn't bear to be cooped up in the hotel anymore, besides, the rain had let up, and Tom was still going around doing atmosphere. So I went out on the street and just walked up to strangers, especially older ones who I thought might remember the minister. And I turned out to have been right.

Of course, Minister Imbach. And one old woman, really ancient, with a walker and all that jazz, told me she reckoned his daughter was now the village pastor. I tried asking her about Wechsler as well, and she thought she knew the name, but had never read anything of his. Ooh no, she says, laughing, as though I'd asked her if she'd ever dived off a ten-meter board. I knew his parents though, she says. Nice people, quiet. His father was a high school teacher. As I already knew.

Home page of the Evangelical Community. Bible verse of the month: You have sown much, and bring in little; You eat, but do not have enough; You drink, but you are not filled with drink; You clothe yourselves, but no one is warm; And he who earns wages, earns wages to put into a bag with holes. Haggai 1:6. Cheery news, isn't it.

As children, we had to learn the books of the Bible in sequence, there was some kind of mnemonic chant, Moses, Joshua and Judges, Ruth and two of Daniel. But Haggai? Where's that—in the Apocrypha somewhere?

Here we are. Contact. Ministry. Three ministers work for the local Evangelical Community. One man and two women. And there she is, Judith Imbach, with picture. What they called a handsome woman, in Wechsler's age. Graying hair, a straight-cut fringe, blue eyes, warm smile. Even her mobile number.

It's five o'clock already, but it's worth a try, ministers are on call all day. A calm, friendly-sounding voice picks up. I say what it's about. A film about Richard Wechsler. A positive silence. Or maybe negative would be more accurate. Silence can be something neutral, but this silence had something drawing or sucking about it, as though it could absorb and engulf words. A kind of vacuum of expectancy.

SHE AGREES to meet me, today, right now. I've explained we're only in the village for a short while. All right, then. Do you want to come by my office? On Kirchgasse. Figures, doesn't it.

Five minutes later, I'm there. I talked about religion with Wechsler on that evening in the café. Extraordinary, the ground you can cover in the space of one or two hours. It was mostly him talking, admittedly, and me listening. But it wasn't the usual old-white-man prattle, explaining the world to us clueless females. I had the sense he was thinking aloud, and I was happy to hear him do it. That was the division of roles: he was explaining himself, I was recording. After all, it's me making a film about him, not the other way around.

He was fascinated by powerful feelings, he said, and where else did you come upon those anymore in the

Western world? In love, in illness and death, and in religion. Sometimes in politics, too, but there it was only
the preoccupation of madmen, and that wasn't interesting. Writing required powerful feelings to fuel it, that was
what kept a story going.

Any kind of feeling?

Any kind of feeling. It just has to be powerful and
uncompromising.

Does he never—like the Swedes—question storytelling itself? I wouldn't mind asking him that. What kind
of book would give you people jumping off a ten-meter
board? It would surely be boring.

Not long ago I read a story of Wechsler's in an an-
thology he gave us. The piece was a detailed description
of a YouTube video. Every word that was spoken, every
little gesture, every facial expression. It was an episode
of *Britain's Got Talent*. Or rather, it was two episodes cut
together, two competitors, two versions of the same fairy
story: the wallflower who becomes a superstar. One was
an unemployed Scots girl, the other was a Welsh mobile-
phone salesman. I've forgotten their names. As a story, I
have to say, it was rather dull.

Then, later, in a different context: he always found
religion faintly embarrassing. That for him was its domi-
nant quality. And yet he couldn't help but be fascinated by
sensible people believing in such things as God, creation,
reincarnation, miracles. Sensible people, who understood
the combustion engine or could do differential calculus,
or cultured people who were well-versed in the classics,

believing in such things. He couldn't get his head around it. I wonder if he had Judith the minister in mind?

I didn't ask him about his faith, nor he about mine. I got the impression God was interesting to him only as an idea, as a kind of variable in his intellectual structure, a character in a story.

God's existence wouldn't change a thing, he said. Before you are born, life is nothing, it's up to you to give it meaning, its value is nothing but the meaning you choose for it. What about another glass of wine?

On my way to see the minister, I see Tom filming a cat. Oh, Tom!

THAT FEELING: as long as we're talking, she won't say anything.

She right away suggested we call each other *Du*, perhaps she thought I was friendly with Wechsler and we were moving in the same circles. But in spite of that, I find her reserved. She wants me to tell her about the film, perhaps she's playing for time.

The concept of the film. Well, indeed, what is the concept of the film? I could quote from the draft proposal for a subsidy: Our film will show Richard Wechsler in his chosen home of Paris and accompany him back to the village where he grew up as a child. We meet his friends and associates and discuss Richard Wechsler's works with literature experts. In longer interview segments, the author will tell us about his writing and his life, and allow us to follow the progress of the novel he is writing, from its first inkling to the completed manuscript. But does that really describe the film we're making? When we asked him questions about his biography, he said: Why do you want to know that? Ask any person on the street, and I bet his life is more interesting than mine. Do you think it's my life that matters? Do you think anyone's life matters? But if not that, then what?

What about the new novel? He doesn't like talking about books he's working on. Then what's his process? In one conversation, I think it was the one down by the river, the day we two later ran away from Tom and Sascha, he talked about his way of working. He never planned anything ahead. He had no idea what was going to happen in a book until the moment he got it down. This was critical— only in this way could a living work come about. It had to grow into the world like something organic. It was a wonderful feeling when a story suddenly turned—like life itself.

If Wechsler were to die, I suddenly think, that would be an unexpected turn all right. Suddenly dropped dead in the middle of our shoot. Fallen under a bus on his way to the station, pushed under a Métro, died of a massive heart attack, stabbed in a mugging. I'd better google him when I get back to the hotel. Maybe that's why he didn't show up today.

We start off by collecting material about him, and his life, talk to him and people who knew him. Then we see what we've got, and try to put it together so it makes sense.

The minister smiles cautiously.

So it makes sense? And what led you to me?

We heard you used to be close. We're looking for people who knew him when he was a young man, before he became a writer.

We heard you two had an affair. As I don't say. Not the way to talk to a woman of the cloth. Not really the way you talk to anyone.

If you were prepared to talk with us, I would let the cameraman know, and we could schedule a short interview with you tomorrow, or even tonight.

Only I don't feel like involving Tom. I want to be alone with her. I like her, I like being in her presence, a quiet, intimate conversation, without the camera's prying eye. I can understand how Wechsler would have been in love with her. If he was.

I look around. The office isn't especially winning, like all offices. Contemporary furniture in pale wood, not much mess, she keeps things straight, a boring but astoundingly robust-looking houseplant, a shelf full of neatly labeled files. Her handwriting is generous. At least there are no Bible verses on the walls, I'm allergic to those. No, she has some rather pleasant landscape photos, presumably the work of an ambitious hobby photographer.

Did you do those?

My husband.

Is he a professional photographer, then?

That was me being flattering. If he'd been a professional, they would have been better pictures. The light gives it away. That, and the quality of the prints.

He teaches shop in the high school. And sports.

At the school where Wechsler's father once taught?

THEY DREW lots for the rooms. There is a brief, awkward moment. All three of the young men are a little in love with her, just as young men are always in love, not really seriously, but still with passion and intensity. Testosterone.

They spent the evening in the restaurant where the butcher worked on his enormous steak. They all had a little bit too much to drink, even Judith. They're all twenty, give or take.

There's only one double bed in the room, more queen than king size. Wechsler gets palpitations when he sees it. Has he slept with a woman before? Maybe. And has Judith slept with a man before? Definitely. She goes into the bathroom first, doesn't take long, comes out wearing a pair of pajamas. Or maybe a nightgown, but nothing glamorous, she doesn't need that at her time of life. And it would probably have embarrassed her. Now it's Wechsler's turn to use the bathroom. It feels odd, slightly intrusive, picturing him as a young fellow. It's none of my business. Never mind.

He's just wearing a T-shirt and undershorts. Judith is already in bed, he lies down beside her, as far from her as he can manage in the narrow bed. She turns off the light. He can't breathe for excitement. Would he dare take the first step? I doubt it. Suddenly he feels a hand on his arm. She says: Whatever happens, we'll remain friends.

AS LONG as she's talking, she won't say anything. So she talks about her high school days with Wechsler, that he always used to read a lot, that he was the class clown, but that there was something secretive about him too. That she was always a little bit scared of him, because he could get so mad. He would feel so insecure, he could be wounding. Instead of telling me he's in love with me, he would make fun of my hair or my clothes. And we used to really have terrible hair and awful clothes. She talks about her teachers, tells anecdotes, all interchangeable. Wechsler was right, his life doesn't tell you much about him. And it's not especially interesting either. Or if it is, then only for him.

Did he have a girlfriend?

She hesitates. It wasn't really like that back then, people didn't pair off. Or very few. We all used to hang around together, I'm sure there were girls who fancied one of the boys, or the boys fancied one of the girls, but there weren't any steady couples in our group.

I wonder.

You have a beautiful church here. A really unusual church.

The change of subject seems not unwelcome to her.

Would you like me to show you around?

She seems to have all the time in the world. I don't mind. Tom's not going anywhere either. When my phone rings, I refuse the call.

I expected her to go on talking, to tell me the history of the church, point out the fin de siècle windows, the unusual color of the pews or the stonework behind the altar, the floral ornamentation, the two angels with their long trumpets. Peace I leave with you, my peace I give to you. But she doesn't say anything at all.

We step into a side entrance, now we're in the nave, silently contemplating the altar and pulpit. The special silence of churches, the tenseness of the echo, in spite of the silence. It feels to me as though the building is quietly breathing in and out. Or is it God's own breathing?

It was just the way it was in his book. She doesn't say so, but I sense it. That night in Paris they made love, and they did it again and again on the following days, all with the vigor and passion of young people, but then nothing came of it. There are no end of reasons for connections to fail or not even properly to come about. He was an ambitious young man moving to Paris, while she was tied to Switzerland by her course and college. She had someone else, he had someone else. There will have been reasons. And then she married the teacher with the happy snaps, and got pregnant and started a family with him. Did she have children? She accepted her first job, did further career development, took other jobs here and there, and then got this one. She will have thought long and hard about going back to the place where she grew up, and then decided: yes. She moved her family into the rectory where she grew up, or they bought a house or rented one. They went on vacation together, made purchases, experienced good times and not-so-good times. And Wechsler all the time was in Paris, writing his books, one after the other, having relationships, about which he hasn't told us a thing, and kept on writing about this one woman, the woman he didn't get. Presumably neither she nor he will tell us any more about it.

So is that the story of our film? A writer repeatedly writing about his garden-variety first love. Is that a reasonable thing? Briefly I ask myself whether Wechsler was using us to find Judith. Could that have been the reason for his no-show: To give us the time to track her down, get in touch with her, on his behalf? But that seems too contrived, he's not so canny as all that. In fact, he's not canny at all, in fact he can be quite slow on the uptake.

I take Judith by the hand, don't ask me why. She seems not to be surprised. She holds me as I hold her. We stand there side by side, hand in hand in silence, for a long time.

TAKE A decision and stick to it, says the young blond woman. Okay?

A young man with short blond hair, blue bathing trunks, and a chain round his neck with what looks like it might be a dog tag in the military looks down into the water from the high board. He scratches his scalp. The young woman beside him is quite well-built, and she's wearing swim shorts like his, only red, and a red-and-white-striped tankini top. Her long, fine hair, lighter than his, falls over her right shoulder. She looks doubtfully, then she smiles. The young man has turned to the woman, he points with both hands at the end of the board.

But I'm not going to do a run-up, that's for sure.

The woman has stepped closer, smiles. She is twisting her fingers.

If I'm jumping, then from here.

Swim over to the ladder and I'll follow, says the woman, gesturing to him which way he should swim after leaping. She looks at him encouragingly.

Are you really going to jump? he asks, and runs his hand through his hair.

Are you going to chicken out?

Maybe.

Both laugh a little sheepishly.

If I see you've hurt yourself, well, not badly, but if you twist your arm or something...

The man raises an arm, as if in illustration of the woman's words.

If you say don't do it, then I won't do it, Frida.

Frida tries to explain her view, moves her hands about in front of her chest, tries to find words. She takes a step in his direction. He looks down into the pool as if hypnotized, and doesn't speak. There's silence for a moment, then Frida asks: Then why did you jump off the five-meter board just a moment ago?

No idea, says the man, pointing down. Look, it's way down there!

He laughs a little incredulously. It's not even high, compared to this one.

Frida puts both her hands to her head and pushes her hair back.

The man steps up to the brink, looks down, and says to himself: All right, Linus, get it over with.

Frida has put her hand to her mouth, as though to chew her fingernails, but she just rubs the backs of her fingers over her lips.

You're doing it for yourself. How do you feel?

I'm just going to tune you out, says Linus.

Okay, okay, says Frida, and takes a step back. Linus quickly turns to her, motions briskly, as though tapping her on the shoulder.

No, no, go on, but you know I'm not really here.

Frida folds her hands. What if I jump first?

No, I want to go first, says Linus resolutely, and lifts his hands preventively. If you don't mind.

Frida smiles appeasingly and gives him an encouraging look. Linus snaps his fingers nervously. I'm sure I'm going to scream like a banshee, he says.

So will I, says Frida.

My knees are shaking, says Linus. He leans forward and props his hands on his knees. Frida copies his movement, then straightens up, lifts one leg behind, holds her ankle in one hand, and then does the same with the other leg.

I was about to jump, and my knees felt it, says Linus.

Frida laughs. There's a hair tie in the water, says Linus, pointing down.

Whoops, says Frida, takes a step toward the edge and looks down too. She swings her hips.

So deciding makes you go weak at the knees?

Eh? Sorry, I wasn't paying attention to you. Though your voice is calming somehow.

Frida takes a deep breath and expels it.

Well...now or never, says Linus.

What, what did we say? asks Frida. If you jump, I have to jump too?

If you fall, I fall too, Frida, says Linus, and looks at her.

She laughs, cocks her foot coquettishly, and folds her hands in front of her bosom. She puts on a mock-tragic expression, and gasps for air, as though sobbing. Okay.

She looks at him with a mix of mockery and emotion, and says very quietly, tenderly: Take care.

I'll see you on the other side, says Linus, facing down. Till we meet in heaven.

Till we meet in heaven, says Frida.

I'm going to do it, Frida.

Yeah, yeah, Frida says enthusiastically. She has balled her hands into fists, shakes them up and down, to pump up Linus. Go for it, wild.

Linus bends his knees a little and jumps. While he's in midair, he's yelling loudly. Frida looks down at the edge from where Linus has leapt. When the splash echoes up, she laughs in relief. She opens out her arms, steps up to the edge, and looks down. She yells and claps her hands once or twice, motions to Linus to get out of the way, moves her mouth silently.

Oh my God, calls Linus from below.

Don't say anything, don't say anything, calls Frida.

She takes a couple of steps back, wipes the hair out of her brow. Then raises both hands like a conductor calling for the orchestra's attention. She takes two rapid steps forward, holds her nose, and leaps.

IF YOU fall, I fall too, Linus said to Frida, presumably it was some sort of joke, but what a line! And: I'll see you on the other side, till we meet in heaven. Do they love each other? Are they destined for one another? Will their love last for the rest of their lives? Or is it just guff? Two young people clowning around in the swimming baths, a filmmaker chats them up, persuades them to get into this existential situation, and now they are standing on the edge of the abyss, and they become aware that all they have is each other. I imagine them standing at the bus stop later, with their hair still damp. They are both quiet, the experience has intimidated them, not their leap, the moments together on the high board. Linus takes hold of Frida's hand, lets it go when the bus comes. Back home, they live in a social housing apartment in a large settlement on the edge of the city, they hang up their wet things in the bathroom to dry, then still silently they make love as though for the very last time. Afterward they lie in bed side by side, and Frida says: I didn't think you'd jump.

They will go on to have children together, move into a larger apartment, their day-to-day life will catch up with them, but never will they forget this evening and this night. They will never tell anyone about it, not even their children, who one day will stand on the three-meter board, and then on the five-meter tower, hesitating, fearful, with wobbly knees. No, this moment is theirs alone. When Linus said: If you fall, I'll fall too.

THE BATHS, another one of those places that keep recurring in Wechsler's books. The swimming baths, the indoor baths, the outdoor baths on Lake Constance, the local ponds dotted about. Did he not miss so much water in Paris, I ask him?

I renounce certain things. One has to be prepared to make sacrifices. It doesn't matter what they are, but they have to be. If you're not prepared to give something up for your work, then you may as well forget about it.

A strange idea. You could sacrifice an animal for each book, I propose, you could slaughter a goat or a chicken. Or at least light a candle in church. I laugh; he doesn't.

There's nothing for free, he says. It may sound batty to you, but I can feel a piece of writing demands not only performance but also sacrifice. The writing is only the sheath that surrounds the sacrifice. Writing without making a sacrifice would be like church without liturgy.

He has sacrificed love, I promptly think, the biggest sacrifice there is. But now he starts laughing too, as though surprised at himself. A strange idea. What will you sacrifice for your film?

Then, later: You can't live in both worlds at once. If you devote yourself to the world of fiction... Think of the amount of time that's taken from your life, all those hours and days and months and years. Maybe that's the sacrifice. Say you had to give one minute of your life for every minute that occurs in your writing…

Then, later: You have no idea how much time a book costs me, not just the actual writing of it, but the waiting for something to happen. And what for? Just words, nothing but words.

He takes a sip of his Ricard.

But you can live in a fictional world and still drink Ricard with me in the real world?

He laughs.

I find pathos pretty repellent, but that's not what it is in his case. He really seems to be at pains to learn something about himself, his life, and his writing. They are thought experiments that no sooner have they been conducted, than he gestures and swats them aside.

Yes, of course, he says. I don't want to portray myself as a hero or anything, a martyr to literature, but increasingly I get the feeling that literature's eating me up, I become a little more transparent with each new book. One doesn't use just one's head and hand to write, one uses the whole of one's body, which eventually gets used up. At the same time, I have the feeling that in the fictive world I'm becoming more and more alive, that books are enough for me, and reality is only there to keep my body going. It's like in that film, *The Matrix*. The red pill or the blue pill.

Which would you choose?

I can't remember which one is which. The fictive world has something very beguiling about it, it fulfills one's every desire. One can't die in it, but one can't live in it either.

Then, later: Sometimes I feel like putting away the laptop and just watching life go on, have experiences, do things, putter about in the garden, travel, have relationships, all that stuff.

But you don't?

He doesn't say anything, but shoots me a dangerous look.

I'm a writer, that's my job.

Would you have had a different life if you'd done something else?

He swats the question away, that's not interesting. If I hadn't written, I wouldn't have been a writer, and you wouldn't be making a film about me. All those other people I might have been are of no interest to you, they don't exist, except possibly in my stories. But you're right, presumably I wouldn't have lived any other way. How did we get onto that? Oh, yes. Anyway, there are swimming baths here too. And you're only two and a half hours away from the sea.

The sea, I say, as though I had just come upon it behind a sand dune.

And he: The sea.

The sea what? Was there anything else? The sea is beautiful? The sea is wild? The sea is primal? No, just the sea, in that rather vanilla voice.

I HAVEN'T heard from him in a long time, says Judith.

Is that true? She lets go my hand, draws a deep breath, and says she had better go, her husband would be wondering where she was.

Mine as well, I say. Boyfriend, actually. My ex-to-be.

Or shall we have a drink together? asks Judith.

A tiny restaurant in a narrow alleyway not far from the church. It would be a nice location. Five or six tables in a dark, wood-paneled room. An old woman is busy behind the bar, and calls out a spirited greeting to us and a rough laugh. Hello, Moni, says Judith, can I get a beer? She turns in my direction with a questioning look.

Same, please.

There used to be a pinball machine outside, Judith says as we sit down. I often played with Richard and the others.

The butcher?

Yes, him too.

He is the only one who knows, and he won't say. Judith won't say. Wechsler won't say. Why should they? What would be the use of saying? What difference would it make? A man and a woman were in love, maybe still are. Is that a film?

Sometimes I'm not sure what really happened and what was just invention, Wechsler said to camera. If you can believe that! But it's a nice excuse, if you don't want to give away anything of yourself.

So is what you write less true than what you lived?

He smiles. No, but it was less consequential.

Is he doing all right? asks Judith.

I have my laptop with me and show her some of the footage, a little edit I made in the hotel. Wechsler walking through Paris. I study her as she watches the film. Her face seems to relax, she smiles.

My God, is that all you have him doing, walking? she asks, and laughs in mock sympathy.

I also asked him how he was feeling. I often start an interview that way, it's a good opening question. How are you feeling? Most people start telling you right away, but Wechsler just said that didn't interest him, that wasn't relevant. He's looking for some image, and moves his hands as though groping for something in a dark room and he doesn't know what. Would you ask a thermometer if it felt cold? he finally asked. And is cold any better or worse than warm? The thermometer shows the temperature, not how it feels about it. No, the comparison's a little off. Once again, he fumbles with his hands. I'm not personally relevant to my fiction, I'm just the eye that sees, the ear that hears, the hand that writes, the body that feels, nothing more. I like the cognomina that unknown artists from the Middle Ages or the Renaissance go by, so that *The Rebellious Angels* is painted by the Master of the Rebellious Angels, or the *Madonna with Violet* by the Master of the Madonna with Violet. When the creator disappears behind the work, and creator and work are inseparable.

I think he's feeling all right.

Judith smiles doubtfully. She was in love with him once, I'm sure of it. She's still in love with him. Even if he doesn't deserve it.

What was the Joyce story that John Huston filmed? Where the man realizes that his wife has been in love with someone else her entire life, a boy who died for her sake a long time ago, who died because he wanted to see her one last time before she went into the convent school. You discover all that in the last few minutes of the film. And then the woman lies crying on the bed, and the man no longer dares to touch her. He stands by the window and looks out, and says to himself what a wretched part I've played in her life. As though I'd never been her husband. What was she like then? What was the girl like whom the boy then was in love with? And it's snowing. Snow is falling on all of Ireland. It is falling over the dark plains of the interior, on the treeless hills, falling softly on the bog of Allen and, farther westward, softly falling into the dark mutinous Shannon waves. Snow is falling gently through the universe, and falling gently as the coming of their final hour upon all the living and the dead. Anjelica Huston plays the woman. Miscast, really. John Huston died before the premiere.

But it's not Judith's husband who interests me, his part is pitiable; and that in spite of the fact he's probably the only one to have behaved decently. No, I'm interested in the two sinners. I can picture them in the hotel in Paris, Judith and Wechsler, both around twenty. It's an inexpensive hotel with a pompous name not far from the station, the décor is a bit tired, with patterned wallpaper, and a yellow cretonne bedspread of doubtful cleanliness. Judith went to the bathroom first. When she returns, she's wearing typical pajamas of the time, cotton jersey, short bottoms, short-sleeved patterned V-neck top. She has already decided to sleep with Richard. Why? Lust? Love? Curiosity? Because she's feeling adventurous? Because the opportunity presents itself? Why wouldn't she want to sleep with him? Her decision is more important than the reasons for it.

When he comes out of the bathroom, she's already in bed, has turned out the overhead light and switched on the bedside lamps. She lies there, but it doesn't seem as though she's tired and wants to sleep. She looks at him expectantly. He is unsettled, goes back in the bathroom, has a drink of water, comes out. He lies down next to her, switches off the lamp on his side, she switches off hers. The only light now is from outside, the only sounds. Quiet traffic noise. He is lying in the dark, not daring to breathe. Then she lays her hand on his arm. Whatever happens, we'll stay friends.

He half rises, leans over her, kisses her. He feels her body through the thin fabric of the pajamas, feels her softness and warmth. She reaches her hands under his T-shirt, pulls it over his head, he takes off her pajama top, her pajama bottoms, her panties. He lies on top of her, she laughs, sighs. The bed creaks. He whispers something. She is louder than he is. Cut.

Are you doing all right? asks Judith. I hold the half-empty glass of beer in my hand, look into it, as though it would tell me my future or her past. She has laid her hand on my arm.

Does a minister have to believe in God?

Not necessarily, she says, but it does help.

HAVE YOU noticed the way they announce the Métro stations in Paris? asks Wechsler. First with rising intonation, like a question: Odéon? Then, when the train's about to stop, the confirmation comes in a disappointed tone: Odéon. When I'm feeling unhappy about something, I sometimes just travel around on the Métro and let that impassive female voice tell me everything's the way it always was, and was meant to be.

Is that true?

No, says Wechsler, laughing, but it's a nice idea. I think on some lines it's a man's voice.

I'm on my way to the swimming baths with Wechsler. It was my idea, I think he thought it was a bit odd. But then he agreed to it. We've been filming for three days, now we have a day off, then we have three more days. It's hot, so why not go to the pool?

I told Tom I wanted to go clothes shopping, which is a foolproof method of getting rid of him. Not completely untrue either. I bought a one-piece bathing suit, I'm too old now to carry off a bikini.

You should forget everything I said yesterday, says Wechsler.

Ségur? inquires the apathetic woman. And then: Ségur.

There's not really much to say about my life. Not much to say about my books either. You can always read them if you want to.

Charles Michels? inquires the woman. Charles Michels.

We have to get off here.

Now it does seem a bit weird to be going swimming with Wechsler. I should at least have been doing it for the film, bringing him to water. Not a pool of course, Wechsler in swimming trunks is not on, that wouldn't be doing him a favor. But maybe the sea, a walk along the beach, that would be better than mountains, less disquieting in the visuals, and much more significance. That way we would have had Paris, the sea, and the village. But could we find room for that in the shooting plan? How far did he say it was to the sea?

We meet behind the changing cabins. I can see he is giving me the once-over, but I take care to look at him too. He is wearing tight shorts that leave little to guesswork, the beginnings of a potbelly, his skin seems very supple, youthful, hairless. He must have seen me looking. It's the law, he says. In all French swimming baths. Loose-fitting trunks are for some reason forbidden.

He lets me go first, and follows right behind as I walk up the steps to the pool. We are almost naked, and yet I don't have the feeling we are any closer now than we were last night in the café. We are just two unclothed bodies. The idea that he's looking at me excites me in spite of that, or maybe just because. The role that water plays in his books isn't something I am going to learn about now.

The ceiling is half-open to the sky, and half the pool is in sunshine, half in shade. All the lanes are full, there are signs on the ends saying Advanced Swimmers, Intermediate Swimmers, Slow Swimmers. We pull on the bathing caps we were issued when we went in, that, too, is obligatory, and we wait for our chance. Wechsler swims fast, but not as fast as I. I sense him trying to put on speed as I draw up alongside, but he gives up, and I pass him.

We're not in the pool for long, we had swum about ten laps when there was the announcement that the pool would be closing in half an hour, it was reserved for the use of school classes in the afternoon. It's hot in the baths, and the water is hot as well, and hardly refreshing at all. The swimmers troop off to the showers, then back down to the changing rooms. For some reason, I can't help thinking of medieval paintings of the Last Judgment, with naked sinners entering the winnowing fire. Before God and in our swimming costumes, we are all alike.

HAVE YOU read his books?

We ask at the same time, and start laughing.

Yes.

Me too. All of them.

Do you like them?

She doesn't reply. Maybe because it's not relevant. I didn't ask her if she likes Wechsler. If you love someone, liking them or not doesn't come into it. Is that nonsense? It sounds like nonsense, but I think it's true. I don't even know if I like Wechsler.

And did you see anything of your youth in his books?

Anyone who lives here recognizes the village. That doesn't matter.

She is evasive, she withdraws. I wish I could make it clear to her that this isn't about the film. But if not that, then what? About truth? There's a big word. Perhaps it's just curiosity. Or I'm trying to win her trust. It would feel like a distinction, a form of intimacy, if she confided in me.

I had a boyfriend once who was a bit like him.

Maybe it'll help her if I talk about myself.

David. I haven't thought about him for ages, wasn't trying to summon him up now, but he seems always to be there as part of what I've become. I sometimes get the sense I'm living my life on a stage in front of all the people I've once known or still know. They're all there, some are closer, some are farther back, maybe one or other of them has already left the theater. Sometimes the lights are up too bright during the performance, and I can hardly see into the auditorium, but I can still feel their presence, hear their laughter, their whispers, a hiss, a spontaneous burst of applause.

David is sitting a long way back. He has a very serious expression on his face. Now he gets up, walks down to the front, climbs the steps onto the stage. He sits down next to me, we're sitting there as for a panel discussion, subject: Andrea and David, the portrait of a failed relationship. I look into the auditorium, in the first row I see Judith, who's smiling up at me encouragingly. Next to her is Wechsler, and a couple of rows behind them are Tom and Sascha, looking like a couple. What makes me think of that? What is there that shows two people are lovers?

David looks at me expectantly.

We weren't lovers, maybe we were lovey-dovey. I don't have much more to say on the matter.

Or: How are you? What are you up to? Are you in a relationship? Do you have children?

But in point of fact, I don't care. And then I notice that David hasn't gotten any older since we broke up. He's exactly the same man I fell in love with and then sent packing. He has the same inquiring glance that made me impatient even then. No, I can't explain it to you, it was just over. These things happen.

Actually, what happened was that I had fallen in love with someone else; perhaps I should have told him. Before David. I had been gone on someone else, but he hadn't been interested, so I took my consolation prize. Then—guess what—the other fellow got interested after all, and it wasn't hard for me to decide. Should I tell David? Best not.

I'm put in mind of what Wechsler said about the great feelings he needs for his books. Presumably I'm not the world champion in strong feelings; I'm pretty pragmatic. A pragmatic hedonist, if there is such a thing. Working on a relationship isn't my thing at all, it sounds too much like hard work. If I don't feel like it, then I don't feel like it, and it can't be helped. For some reason I just didn't fancy David anymore, while I did fancy the other fellow. And then that didn't last very long, so it was probably a mistake. That was the guy who was madly jealous, and who now does tai chi or chi gong or shiatsu, I can't tell them apart.

My pride wouldn't let me go back to David. I wonder if he would have taken me back?

The end of a story. But how did it begin? Was I really already in love with the other fellow? David was shy, quiet, a loner, that's maybe what reminded me of Wechsler. Did I perhaps feel sorry for him? Or did I sense he had powerful feelings? Was that what drew me to him? Was I in love not with him, but with his love? And was he perhaps also more in love with love than with me? That great love that set us apart from the others, that made us unique. He wrote me letters, even though we saw each other almost every day, he came bearing presents. He thought about how to delight me. He was altogether rather thoughtful—perhaps too much so. Things weren't straightforward with him, to begin with I liked that, then I lost patience with it. He said he was addicted to me. When I left him, I felt I was punishing him, and took a strange pleasure in hurting him. This isn't something I'm proud of, but that's the way it was.

MY FAITH is at its strongest when we're singing, I remember Judith saying to me in the church. Faith is probably the wrong word. Then God is simply present. Like a feeling. A feeling of being sheltered.

We've gone for a stroll up the mountain, though it was already dark. We walk up past the church, go by a few single-family homes, villas, an orchard. One last farmhouse, and we're out of the village, and are among fields, meadows, and forest. There are no more streetlights out here, but the moon is bright enough to see by. And now at last Judith starts talking, but not really talking to me, talking to herself, describing her memories to herself. Some of it I don't hear, because it's too softly spoken, and I don't ask her to repeat anything for fear it might make her stop. I just let her talk.

It's an extraordinary story, no writer would dare offer anything like it in a work of fiction. Suddenly I can see parts of it in all Wechsler's books, elements, fragments, variations. The powerful feeling that makes me, frankly, a little envious.

Judith stops. We are some way up the mountain already, looking down at the village lights. In every one of them there's a story, behind every illuminated window. And where the windows are dark, dreams are growing, yet more stories. It's spring, a moonless night in the small town, starless and Bible-black . . .

You are his muse, I say.

She laughs. Is that what I want? Would you like to be a muse? But one probably has little say in the matter.

Do you regret what you did?

Not for a moment.

She's pretty cool for a minister.

You are his victim. I didn't say that. But I did wonder who suffers more, the victim or the sacrifice. And I'm not talking chickens or goats here.

Judith laughs. She comes over as a young, exuberant woman, though she must be almost sixty. Don't they say reform church minister is the healthiest profession? Or was it the unhealthiest? It was one or the other.

It's just a possibility, she says.

Meaning what? And: she didn't tell me everything. You can never tell everything. The hours and days they spent together, the excitement, the caresses, the sex. The meetings and partings, the joy and despair. One possibility? One version of the story? And what would be Wechsler's version? What would be mine? Our film is supposed to show the truth, but I gradually begin to question that, and question whether such a truth even exists. Even the little I know of the truth is such that I can't show it. That would be the stories you tell yourself when the lights are out, when there are two of you or even only one of you. In the light, they fade away.

I imagine her visiting him in his house in a Parisian suburb. She said he doesn't have to collect her, it's not the first time she's going to see him. He would have gladly done it, but she doesn't want him to, she knows what she wants. She wants to ring his doorbell, wants him to open the door to her, as though she were the lady next door, come for a natter, or the postie with a parcel. They look each other in the eye, and she takes a step forward. For the first half hour, neither speaks, they kiss, embrace, undress.

Then they are lying together side by side, slowly recovering their calm, exchanging their first words, How was the journey? She tells him about her daughters, he tells her about a meeting with his publisher, blah, all of it blah, none of it matters.

There is the truth of the senses, the sensations they give us, smell, taste, touch, the feeling of a hand over a shaved neck, through thick hair, pushing away a strand, warmth and cold, softness and firmness.

For the rest of the day they don't put their clothes on. At most, Judith might put on her slip, a little cardigan, because it's cool indoors, she doesn't even do it up, her breasts are freely visible in it. He takes it off her anyway. They embrace. They lie together under the duvet, start touching again, they can't get enough of one another. Eventually, they need to eat. And always that desire that won't be appeased and therefore can't stop.

Judith didn't tell me anything.

TOM IS out when I return to the room. On the bed is a list with the names of pasta varieties, there must be at least fifty of them. Did he really think of them all by himself? Or did he cheat and google them? Do I owe him an ice cream?

I google pasta varieties myself. If Tom did cheat, he at least didn't do it from Wikipedia. It turns out there aren't just pasta shapes but whole genuses and species of pasta, hollow, short, long, fresh.

Sascha was due to arrive this afternoon. We planned two days for preliminary interviews and general filming in the village, and then three for proper takes, interviews with proper sound, and so forth. Wechsler walks through the village, meets people from his past, one of his teachers, old friends, that kind of thing.

The teacher he described as most significant for his development unfortunately isn't alive anymore. I found the other one he mentioned, but he had very little to say for himself. In fact: he said exactly what you expected him to say. I got the impression he couldn't actually remember Wechsler, and simply said what he thought was plausible: eager student, articulate, funny, empathetic. He was clearly proud that Wechsler had studied with him, and no doubt reckoned he had played a part in his success. Had he read Wechsler's books? Oh, that was something he had been meaning to do for a long time, yes, he must get around to it one day. I thought it was better not to tell him what Wechsler had said about him.

I send Sascha a WhatsApp message, she doesn't get back to me. I call down to reception and ask if she's checked in. I get her room number and call her. Sascha picks up.

Hello, Sascha.

Hello, Andrea.

Get here all right?

Oh, yes. She sounds a little uncertain, hesitant.

Have you got Tom with you?

Another brief hesitation. Yes, he was showing me the footage. We had a brief talk about how we might . . .

Okay. Will you come down?

It takes them a long time.

Crisis meeting. What do we do in the event that Wechsler doesn't show up? Sascha refers to Tom as Thomas. It's all Thomas this, Thomas that. Is it possible that the two of them...? It seems I've caught the habit of not finishing my sentences. Perhaps it's that I don't want to, I don't want to think it through to the end. Even though, in point of fact, it would be the ideal solution and I'd be rid of him. Nevertheless, the thought offends me. The little slut! I can't think of a matching term for him, but it wouldn't exactly surprise me if he... Young woman he can impress, who listens patiently to his stories, without saying: I've heard that a hundred times already. Sure, and then throw in the fact that she's ten years younger, that's not a disadvantage either. It would free me, which is a thought I'd need to get used to.

EASE, SPEED, precision, clarity, layerings. Those are just suggestions, not rules or laws. I like that. I even like the word: suggestion. Can I make a suggestion, this is just a suggestion. I downloaded the book at some point, but I've never read it.

My work consisted primarily of taking away weight; I strove to take the weight from human beings, from heavenly bodies, from cities; but most of all I tried to take weight from the language and structure of a story.

I was unable to sleep and went downstairs and sat in one of the chairs in the lobby. The night porter showed up, a cute-looking boy who's presumably paying his way through college by night work, and who reckoned he could earn a wage by sleeping. No dice. He looks exhausted, but nevertheless asks me if I'd like a drink. Beer or coffee? It's three a.m., so are we night or morning? You don't start a day with beer, but I could conceivably call it a nightcap. Maybe it'll help me get to sleep. Besides, the coffee machine has surely been cleaned and switched off.

A beer would be nice.

I flick through one of the glossy magazines left out on the coffee table. Art by the lake. The charming villa in Ticino where an art dealer couple found an appropriate setting—for themselves and some of their most beautiful *objets*. Happiness is a sun-drenched garden. At home in a large country estate. Within these old walls a lady photographer has carved out a rural retreat for herself. Her large country garden is a lot of work, but gives her endless delight. I was feeling uninspired and thought a natural setting would provide the ideal antidote to weekday stress, says forty-eight-year-old independent lady photographer. Tell me about it.

The night porter brings me my beer, and seems chatty and at a loose end. How did I like it here? Was I on business? Was I on my own? Is he flirting with me? It would be somewhat ridiculous, given that he's half my age, if you can trust appearances. I give evasive replies. I prefer to ask the questions myself rather than give answers, so it's my turn: Has he been working here for long? Does he enjoy the work? What does he do in the daytime?

He's studying German, and was working all summer as a night porter, the new semester was about to begin next week, then he'll just work occasional weekends. Yes, he likes the job, it leaves him plenty of time for reading. Has he come across Wechsler? Heard the name, but never read anything by him. What authors does he like, then? Poets of the Baroque. Really? Are they even a thing? He gives a little lecture: morbidity, carpe diem, the Thirty Years' War.

Baroque poetry! Isn't it weird how the proponents of the most abstruse disciplines persuade themselves that their studies are somehow central. I once came across a book about zootomy in a secondhand bookshop. Zootomists engage in the study of animal remains, ascertaining if they are related, and so forth. I just looked at the book because I liked the illustrations. In the introduction, the man declared more or less that zootomy was the mother of the sciences.

So here we are with Baroque poetry: an epoch of contradictions. The Thirty Years' War raging over half the continent. Bubbling joie de vivre encounters the obsession with mortality. When did all this happen? More or less the entire seventeenth century. So the years starting with sixteen. I don't know squat about those. This world and the next, virtue and desire, eroticism and ascesis. It sounds funny, hearing those big concepts from the mouth of this student. How much does a twenty-year-old know about desire? Frivolity and earnestness, terrestrial life against heavenly life. And then he starts to recite a poem:

What are the myriad objects of our desire
But ignis fatuus, Saint Elmo's fire.
What is the life of humankind
But the fantastic imagining of time?

I bet he writes poems himself, but I decide not to ask him in case he shares those with me as well.

As night porter, you probably witnessed some shenanigans?

He ducks the question, he seems still carried away by his little lecture. He has to do his rounds now.

Would you mind if I went with you?

He's clearly unhappy in my company. He doesn't know if it's allowed, and at his age, people still like to abide by rules. But why should it be forbidden? And who would catch us? The notion of wandering around a dark hotel with a young man has captivated me, but after just a few minutes, I'm bored of trotting along after him and listening to his commentaries. What do I care where empty containers are stored? Where the heating plant is, where the passage is to the garage? I'd rather have a little more Baroque, frankly. I'm annoyed to have got us into this situation. Sometimes I overdo it.

Have you got a girlfriend?

He seems not to have noticed that I'm using the intimate *Du* with him. He continues to call me *Sie.* When he holds a door open for me for the tenth time, I graze his arm with my hand and smile at him. He lowers his glance, is he staring at my breasts, or is he coming over all shy? He blushes furiously. But why am I saying all this? It's got nothing to do with Wechsler and our film. And Tom has nothing to reproach me with. We're fifteen–all, level-pegging. Deuce. Whatever. Later, I was able to get to sleep.

JUDITH HAS two children, both girls. She would have pre-ferred boys. She must be the first woman who has said that to me. Normally they all say, It's perfect the way it is, a boy/girl is the best thing that could have happened, I can't imagine it any other way. But Judith can imagine plenty, I noticed that right away.

She had her children relatively late, her girls are both in their teens, though still under twenty, she did tell me the ages, but I forgot. At any rate, she was about my age when the children were born. They're both in high school, one is about to graduate, and they both have strikingly unbiblical names, Ann and Ella. I wonder what they would say if they knew... I'm thinking one of them may be Wechsler's—perhaps both. There are apparently more mailman's children than is commonly thought.

I google mailman's child. The worldwide figure is around two percent. Still. Among the Yanomami it's closer to ten percent. Now, who are the Yanomami again? A case for Dr. Google. Indigenous people living in the 1,500-meter-high Serra Parima on the borders of Vene-zuela and Brazil, between the Orinoco and the Amazon. Also known as Yanomama and Yanomamo. Warlike in outlook, but afraid of crossing deep water. Well, no reason to fear them, then. But they're a bit more interesting than pasta varietals. Where was I?

As we were driving up to the village we stopped at a small lake where Wechsler and his friends often used to go swimming when they were all kids. He told me about it in Paris. I made a note of the name and saw from the map that it's more or less on our way. This lake crops up in many of his books, once a couple make love there for the very first time, another time two friends bike there at night, bathe naked, and then something dramatic happens, and one of them loses his life.

The lake lay in a valley between two villages and was maybe a kilometer long. It was ringed by some narrow woods, in a few places the shore was grown over with rushes. At one end there was a bathing place with changing cabins, a kiosk, a barbecue spot, and even a swimming raft. When we arrived, there was no one there, and the entrance was open. We sat down in the meadow and looked across at the water.

A beautiful spot, isn't it, said Tom.

Do you feel like a swim? I took a few steps down to the waterline and dipped my hand in. It's not cold.

But Tom didn't care for water that much. He liked beer better, he would say sometimes, and think he was being hilarious. He suggested coming here with Wechsler, and framed a view with his two hands as though to suggest a shot, it must be something he cribbed from some famous director.

We have the sun going down, and he's sitting on the grass looking out over the water, and we get an actor to read the passages from his books. A bit of music, a bit of sparkle on the water.

Sounds super.

And then on to the village, which turns out to be farther than I thought. It was almost half an hour by car. And yet they cycled there at night in Wechsler's book? Stretches credulity.

THE CRISIS meeting didn't solve anything. Wechsler will come or he won't. Tom has banged Sascha or he hasn't. The film is going to be made or it won't. Ignis fatuus.

Did I not want children? Wechsler asked me when we had lunch together after our swim. Or rather I had lunch, he just ordered coffee.

What about you?

He again didn't answer, but then I hadn't answered either. Is it that the books are his children? No, he didn't care for that metaphor, he thought it was pretentious. Children are children, and books are books. He found the notion of having children a strange one—one more thing that he found strange. Even the verb seemed wrong to him, do you have children in the sense of having a house or a car or a dog? But no better expression came to his mind.

I imagined being Wechsler's daughter. Would it feel different? Presumably he would interfere in my life, give me advice, be proud of me or disappointed, depending on my progress. He would be worried about me, and he wouldn't like Tom, because fathers never like their daughters' beaux. At least that's what they say. He would be sad that we would be losing touch, and yet unable to do anything about it. And what about me? I would endure him, maybe love him. He would be familiar to me. I would know what he spends his days doing, what his habits are, what his smell is like, what he looks like in underpants. I wouldn't read his books. Afterward, I would be sad that we hadn't had more of a life in common. Would I call him Papa? Or by his first name, Richard? He would certainly offer to pay for our meals together. As is the case now.

You don't have to.

No, I don't have to.

He told me an elaborate story about always being paid for when he was a young author, and now…nothing important.

Incidentally, Tom doesn't need to know that we were swimming together, all right?

Sure, says Wechsler, and winks at me, as though we'd been to bed together.

Then we walked along the Seine, silent most of the time, that was nice. I had the feeling he liked me, in a very discreet, reticent way. I liked him too.

That night I had a dream about Wechsler. We were eating together in some unspecified place that felt both private and public, maybe an ambassador's residence or a rich patron's home. Wechsler had cooked our dinner and brought it along. I see him walking up the stairs with dishes full of food, and I see he's in pain. His knees are hurting him. We sit down on a kind of terrace at a nicely laid table, with nice porcelain and silver and silver candle-holders. We eat and talk. He is telling me about a young man who is full of fears, he describes everything in great detail, but I can't remember what the young man was so afraid of. The possibility of freedom, perhaps?

It's gotten dark on the terrace, the candles are flickering, light comes out from inside the house. It begins to rain. We could go inside, but we stay where we are. The rain is a warm summer rain, and in next to no time we're sopping wet, but we carry on eating and talking, as though nothing were the matter. Then we walk through a park with old trees. We're barefoot, I'm carrying my shoes in my hands, they are exquisitely made designer things with high heels, I have never owned anything like that, nor would I ever wear them, but in my dream, I love these shoes more than anything. The earth is sodden and soft, it's like a mire in which we're sinking. We wade through the water, first up to our ankles, then up to our knees. The hem of my dress touches the water. What am I doing in a dress? I hardly ever wear dresses. It must be silk, it feels smooth, cool, slinky. I slow down, hold my shoes high over my head to protect them. Wechsler comes up to me from behind, takes me round the waist. It was a beautiful dream, and I was happy beyond dreams.

NO SOONER have I finally fallen asleep than Tom wakes me. It feels like I've been asleep for about ten minutes. I'm going to write a book myself now. About what assholes men are. About what an asshole Tom is. Something to give him a slap in the face. Even that would be too generous.

We are breakfasting with Sascha. She's all done up to the nines, well, she's washed her hair. And she's brought down all her gear into the breakfast room, no idea why. Does she think it makes her look cool? Or is she meaning to get started right away? Or leave? I wouldn't mind.

Tom and Sascha are playing at being normal and being professional. They are talking in extra-loud voices about microphone brackets and plug connections. It sounds pathetic, I don't understand this game. Maybe they've sensed my suspicion. I don't pay any attention to them and just read the newspaper.

In a book review in the arts section, there's a sentence: How can you write about a life? As a movement from an unknown source to an ever-more-blatant ending? Some Swede wrote that. Another Swede. What is it with these Swedes all of a sudden? There aren't even all that many of them, all told. Then there's a report about gangs in Göteborg. There seems to be something rotten in the state...no, that was Denmark.

So: from an unknown source to an ever-more-blatant ending? Is that right? Maybe we keep our backs turned to the past? The past changes, we can manipulate it, but not the future. And least of all the end, because it never slips into the past.

Nothing much happens in the village. Wechsler hasn't shown up, and he hasn't got in touch either. We conducted a couple of interviews, captured some atmosphere, cats and dogs, birds, the school, the pub, the forest, the river. We even filmed the vineyards, the grapes are not yet ripe, but no one will see that. I called Judith to see if we can meet again. She has no time, she has a funeral to prepare for. I don't know if that's actually true or not. Maybe she was upset about confessing to me.

I gave Tom the third degree, he denies everything, he says I'm paranoid. He has never had anything with Sascha, and wasn't proposing to either. She wasn't even his type.

And what if she were your type? Would you take up with her then?

I'm unfair. Maybe he's telling the truth and I'm imagining everything. If I were him, I would certainly be having an affair with her, the way I'm treating him. But he is not me. We check out. We can forget about the film. It's over.

II

BAGNEUX? BAGNEUX.

Bourg-la-Reine? Bourg-la-Reine.

Parc de Sceaux? Parc de Sceaux.

I never noticed that, says Judith.

I wouldn't have noticed it either, if Richard hadn't pointed it out to me.

Now that he's no longer around, I've taken to calling him Richard. As though we had grown closer since his death. And have we? At any rate, he can't avoid me any longer. But then he doesn't give me any more answers either. The last word has been spoken, so to speak. The dice have been thrown. No, that doesn't fit.

We get off at the next stop, says Judith.

In the village, I had briefly supposed that the reason Wechsler wasn't coming was because he had suddenly died, but of course that wasn't the case. As a rule, people don't die suddenly, or not when you're expecting it or dreading it. We had gone on having dealings for a while, the whole thing was a pretty sordid story. He had signed

an agreement, Richard Wechsler, hereinafter known as
The Author hereby, blah-blah, blah-blah. The Author de-
clares himself willing to participate in this film project for
no payment, and during the creation of His Next Work, to
be accompanied and filmed by a camera team. And so on
and so forth. Details (in particular the number of shooting days, the locations, individual scenes, et cetera) to be
worked out in an ongoing manner by agreement with both
parties.

That was the rub, the ongoing manner, it could mean
anything. We had talked about the shooting plan, and to
begin with Wechsler had participated and stuck to his side
of the agreement. Why wouldn't he, after all? My word
is my bond. But then...The material from Paris wasn't
enough for a film, not even technically. The producer was
forced to repay the grant money, she was left with the ex-
penses, our own wretched fees were canceled. She wanted
to sue Wechsler, but her lawyer advised against it. What
good would it have done? A long legal wrangle, bother,
costs. Would we have ever seen any money at the end of it?

He never came up with any justification. I wrote him a
couple of emails, first hopping mad, then later just asking
for some kind of explanation. Why? Silence. Maybe the
fatal illness had set in by that time. What is it they say?
After a long, heavy illness, which he/she bravely bore, and
still full of plans for the future, he/she was taken from his/
her active life.

Following the disaster with Wechsler, I struggled on
for almost another two years. I split with Tom, that was

the easiest part of the new beginning, at least for me. After that, I had one or two irons in the fire, female subjects, but none of them was realized. My savings melted away. Eventually I understood that I couldn't go on like this, and I started looking for a job. But there's nothing I can do, and who wants a failed filmmaker with no degree and questionable social skills? I quickly abandoned the idea of becoming a cemetery groundskeeper when I saw what a pittance they earned; to work for the post office meant getting up at five, which was out of the question for a night owl like me. I was lucky finally to land an office job in the marketing wing of a large insurance company. They seemed to like me there, God knows why. I was due to begin there in the middle of October, when the woman who was going to show me the ropes was due back from maternity leave. That was fine by me, a few more weeks of freedom. So, next, the short vacation with Judith.

WE DIDN'T talk much on the train. Judith read, I watched YouTube videos. For unknown reasons, I've recently had loads of recommendations of features on serial killers, no idea what that's about. I've never ordered butcher's knives or cable ties online or other stuff you might need if you were going to be a serial killer, and I haven't googled the subject either. I'm not interested in serial killers. But for some reason I got stuck on the subject. You don't learn a whole hell of a lot. There's always a female journalist sitting in a narrow interview room, and some figure in prison clothes opposite her. The journalist always seeks cautiously and respectfully to learn what makes a murderer, but the murderer doesn't know the answer. They have a way of looming into the camera, they lean forward as though to grab the viewer by the throat, and then they talk about their murders the way other people might talk about an evening with friends or a weekend outing with the family. Some seem aggrieved with how everything's turned out, how they're in prison now, are only allowed one shower a week, are maybe facing the electric chair, it's all so unfair. Often they laugh, because they're amazed by what they've done. Then wow, I like cut her throat. The journalists are often Australian women, there's evidently some interest there in serial killers. Something we don't have in common. Well, there are a few others besides. For instance, I'd never eat kangaroo, and I would never dare drive on the left, not even on a bicycle. And then the connection breaks, and I've used up my available data.

I pick up the newspaper. Someone's written something on Proust, more particularly on why he doesn't read Proust. Or he started reading Proust, and then gave up. Myself, I've never read Proust. I'm not interested. But I'm even less interested in why others aren't interested, and less still in why others, having been interested once, no longer are. And yet I read the article. And copy down a sentence I like from it…When I claim I have an existence outside myself; that day in and day out I leave myself, and will sooner recognize myself in others than others in myself. That sounds grand, I think. It asks to be put to music, lofty, hymnal music.

I sneak a look at Judith, try to make out the title of the book she's reading. She must have noticed me, because she turns the book round and holds it out: Gershom Scholem, *Major Trends in Jewish Mysticism*. Huh. I suppose that's the kind of thing a minister is bound to read.

Richard gave it to me, she says, but I've never read it. He didn't either. He said, I expect it's more in your line.

She smiles. Here, listen:

When the Baal Shem had a difficult task before him, a secret task for the benefit of creation, he would go to a certain place in the woods, light a fire, and meditate in prayer—and what he had set out to perform was done.

When a generation later the "Maggid" of Meseritz was faced with the same task he would go to the same place in the woods and say: We can no longer light the fire, but we can still speak the prayers—and what he wanted done became reality.

Again a generation later Rabbi Moshe Leib of Sassov had to perform this task. And he went into the woods and said: We can no longer light a fire, nor do we know the secret meditations belonging to the prayer, but we do know the place in the woods to which it all belongs—and that must be sufficient; and sufficient it was.

He would have liked that, says Judith. I wonder what it was: a secret task for the benefit of creation?

Telling stories? I suggest.

WE MET up again at the funeral. I learned about Wechsler's death in the newspaper. There were two death announcements, one from his publisher, the other from his family, with a nice if somewhat nihilistic chant:

The world goes on its way,
The people come and go,
As though you'd never been,
As though nothing had passed.

IN THE arts section a couple of days later, there was a brief tribute, no photo, a single column. A quiet but distinct voice, died in the city that was his adopted home, and then something about light and rooms and atmospheres. It was written by a reviewer who had never liked him and who regularly panned his books. Wechsler had once complained about him in a rare display of self-pity, and I had said so. Yes, he said, it's an aspect of me I don't like either. And he changed the subject.

Then, later: There are moments in company when I really don't like myself. I think the people with me failed to notice it, I was behaving more or less in the way they expected, but it didn't feel like me, I wasn't being honest. Strangely enough, those moments of deceit and disguise were my most successful. But every so often there would be someone there who would look me in the eye and give me the feeling they were onto me. I didn't see contempt in the way they looked at me, at most gentle mockery. But my embarrassment in front of this person weighed more with me than the success I had with the others.

And what was your way out of this fix?

I would withdraw into myself and avoid such situations altogether.

I LIKE the word eulogy. You speak well of someone, there's a Latin phrase about that, and maybe on the bounds of life and death, in that white light that people have reported seeing who have gone up to the brink, they hear you. Wechsler would turn in his grave if he could hear me. To him the idea of life after death was unhygienic, he once said. No, not unhygienic, unesthetic. In the same way as sequels of every hit film that you get nowadays are rarely as good as the original. Except *The Godfather*, I said, Part II is at least as good as Part I. Well, maybe, he said, but there's to be no sequel to my life, it has a distinct beginning and ending. And it's no better or worse than it has to be. And was it good, then? I asked. He thought about it for a moment, and said, yes, it was good, very good, even.

What was that again? From an unknown source to an ever-more-blatant ending. Wechsler saw his end ahead of him. We talked about it. But first, his funeral:

It was easy enough to find out where and when it was taking place. I can't tell you why I went. It was as if we had unfinished business. What was strange was that they brought Wechsler back to Switzerland, after all his years in France. I wonder if that was his wish? And what about the village? The people and the plants and the soil all harbor a bit of you, and even if you don't know it, it's there waiting for you. Is that true? Isn't it the other way around, that there's a bit of the village, the people, the plants, and the soil in you? Well, anyway, they brought him home. A piece of him, the mortal remains, as they say. Not sure how I feel about that. All of us is mortal, and what's left over aren't remains, it's the whole thing. Unless you believe in immortality, anyway.

Judith conducted the service, not in the church but in the cemetery chapel, a rather progressive structure from the fifties or sixties. I wonder what she was going through. I kept waiting for her to burst into tears, but she was too much of a pro for that. She spoke rather impressively about Wechsler and his books, and there was something from Scripture as well, but it was measured and not too much of it, something from the Old Testament, which was Wechsler's preference as well. I must ask her what the passage was. The music was very nice too, Bach, never wrong. And there was singing as well, "O God, Our Help," and something else I've forgotten.

AT THE end of the service, the mourners trooped outside, while the organ noodled around on a Bach chorale, as though unable to find its way out. People stood around seeming just a little lost. It was early September, one of those bright, cool days, with a breeze and very clear air, the light seeming somehow Scandinavian. There weren't many people in attendance, but not so few that it was embarrassing either. He had always steered clear of mass occasions, Wechsler said once, and he was getting his payback for it now. One group clumped together, that was probably family, siblings, did he have siblings, nieces and nephews, cousins, what do I know, I can't remember the names in the death announcement. Our dear—what did they call him? Brother, uncle, father, son, cousin? They looked pleasant enough, a little subdued, yes, but nothing ostentatious about them. No one was sobbing loudly or breaking down over the coffin the way they do in bad films. He was a decent enough man, apart from wrecking our documentary and my career. Then there were some people from the village. I recognized the butcher and the former teacher because we had interviewed them. A couple of people seemed officious and were in dark suits. Local politicians, maybe? Or people from the publishers? Two giggly little girls, probably their first funeral, so they were rather excited. Nice. Wechsler would have liked that.

Judith spoke first to the family, saying hello and shaking hands in various quarters. They all looked as though they were saying she had done well. Was the man she seemed to avoid possibly her own husband, the teacher-cum-photographer? He looked pleasant enough as well. Not much in the way of hair, but pretty fit looking. Then she must have seen me. I was standing on the periphery, next to a peacefully burbling fountain. There was another fountain in the schoolhouse, no idea why that should come to mind now, it seemed unusual to me but nice, a quietly burbling fountain just inside the entrance of a school. Everything seemed to be in a state of festive calm and beauty just now, not sad at all. Bearing out the truth of evanescence, people coming, people going.

Judith gave me a quick hug that felt both casual and sincere, then stood next to me, and we looked at the group together. That's the mayor, she said, pointing to one of the men in dark suits, in animated conversation with two others. I don't think he's ever read anything of Richard's, but it's nice of him to turn up, don't you think? The man he's talking to is the culture secretary, and the third is the parish clerk. That group over there went to school together. I don't know the lady with the dog.

Do they allow dogs in the cemetery? I thought of all the bones, but didn't say anything. Might have been a bit disrespectful.

Is that man over there your husband?

She didn't answer.

How things come to an end. All the excitement, the endeavor, the struggle, the illnesses and therapies, operations, sleepless nights, slight improvements and sudden reverses. Then death, autopsy, cause of death, paperwork, notification of the authorities, signatures on forms. And then it's just over, and we're left to stand there on a sunny day in September, thinking of him a bit before going home.

But there's nothing really sad about it.

I know what you mean, she says. But it is sad, very sad.

JUDITH IS turning the pages of her book while we're racing across the plains of France at two hundred miles an hour. Another two hours and seven minutes until we arrive. Trains used to make this somniferous clattering noise, dadadadum, dadadadum, but ever since they started welding the rails, an engineer once told me, you just hear an even rumble, so a TGV sounds a bit like a washing machine. There ought to be a soundtrack you can download, train sounds, and you could take your pick among European, Trans-Siberian, and American; with the American track, you'd get the wail you hear on films as well, whoo whoo, and then maybe cable railway, rack railway, maybe streetcar as well.

I've just taken receipt of some new data capacity, courtesy of SNCF. Just like that. Thank you, thank you. Next: of course it exists, train noises on the Internet. All you could ask for. Ten hours through the wintry taiga of Siberia. And you hear the old sound: dadadadum, dadadadum. And outside the frozen windows nothing changes, not even the light. Dadadadum, dadadadum, dadadadum, dadadadum, dadadadum. Don't think I watched all ten hours, I skipped about, maybe I missed a little guardhouse or a ptarmigan or a railroad switch, but I don't think so. Someone called Sergey uploaded it, and it's had 109,000 views. Thank you too, Sergey. I stopped the video after a couple of minutes. Perhaps a new serial killer?

I look across to Judith. She seems to have dropped off, Jewish mysticism can't have been as exciting as all that.

The book is on her lap, her eyes are shut, her face has relaxed. She is a good-looking woman, very natural, very little makeup, almost unnoticeable. Her clothes are casual but tasteful. Sandals, linen pants, sleeveless linen top. If I were a man, I'd think she was sexy.

I try to picture her as a girl. Probably not so very different. No gray hair, of course, maybe a little slimmer, and with one of those awful haircuts we all had back then. A bubble perm. In the eighties, girls looked much older than they do now, just as well I was only just born then.

BECAUSE YOU liked him, Judith said. And because no one else knows. About him and me.

No one? Really?

Ten days after the funeral, she called me to ask if I felt like going to Paris with her. She wanted to see Wechsler's house.

Do you mean break into it?

I've still got a key, she said.

Richard told her she could come anytime, so it wasn't really housebreaking. And she wasn't going to take anything that didn't belong to her.

Photos? Letters? Do you mean to destroy evidence? I had to laugh. Pretty cool, this lady.

There was never a crime, so it's not evidence, she said. Anyway, my husband...

Someone else who doesn't finish her sentences. Had she spoken to her husband? Was she going to acknowledge

Wechsler, now that he was dead and buried? Had her husband forgiven her? Or left her? Would she leave him now, though it no longer made any sense to do so? At any rate, she wanted me to go with her to Paris.

Sure, I said. When were you planning to go?

WHEN WE get out at Sceaux, I can't help but feel a little tired, first the TGV train, then the suburban RER, and perhaps some of the frisson of doing something forbidden as well.

It looks very different here than in the city, more air, more light, more greenery, much less noise.

There's a Monoprix farther along, says Judith, we always used to buy our groceries there.

I haven't had anything proper to eat all day; even so, I can't think of anything I really feel like eating in the store. So, fallback position: spaghetti and tomato sauce.

I have a good recipe for the sauce. Canned tomatoes, one large onion cut in half, lots of butter, no salt, no spices; keep at a steady simmer, take out the onion, and that's your sauce.

Fine by me, says Judith. She buys a few other things, bread, because in France you always buy bread, salad for a good conscience, water, a couple of bottles of wine.

We can eat out sometime as well, she says, I know there used to be a Thai restaurant here, and an Italian and a sushi place.

And what if they've gone and changed the locks?

Why would they do that?

It's a quiet street, with a kink in the middle. There is very little traffic, and no pedestrians. The gardens are all overgrown, in places you can hardly see the houses anymore, just feel them somewhere in all the foliage. Some are imposing and well-kept, others look neglected, and there are a couple of new builds in there as well, though they don't look new, more a kind of timeless old-fashioned. Then we're standing in front of Wechsler's house. It's almost a cube. A drive leads down to the underground garage, a concrete-slab path goes from the garden gate to a flight of steps, up above there's a terrace along one whole side of the house, with a little metal table, three collapsible chairs in poor condition, a deck chair. The extensive grounds are ringed by a tall, ivy-clad brick wall, in the lee of which a few stringy hydrangeas are growing. The lawn is stringy too, the grass high in places, in others you see the bare ground. There's a big cedar in front of the house, a sycamore to the side, and some smaller trees, maybe wild cherries or bird cherries. I've stopped at the foot of the steps, while Judith is fiddling with the lock upstairs. When she's got it open, she looks to me, waits for me to join her, and we walk inside together. Does she need a witness? I am tempted to take her hand again.

It probably smells this way in any house that's been left unoccupied and unaired for a few weeks. A bit stale, but not unpleasant. A warm smell of cloth and dust and wood.

AT FIRST we talk in whispers, as though we were scared of being caught. But who can hear us, who would come by? The dispute about the inheritance is unresolved, Richard's sister told Judith, lines have been drawn, even though the matter's pretty clear. Luckily, her brother wrote a will. A good portion of his estate would be taken in tax. And they would have to go to Paris at some point to clear the house. Or perhaps have it cleared by a firm of specialists. All the papers would probably be shipped to the national literary archive in Bern, talks were ongoing, and the rest would be thrown out.

You have to picture the house a little like that in John Huston's *The Dead*, strange the way I keep returning to that film. It must have made a big impression on me, even though it was years ago that I saw it. An evening party on Epiphany at the house of two old sisters, who invite family and friends every year on that day. They talk about politics, religion, Ireland and England, someone recites a poem, there is singing and dancing. Then one of the old sisters sings a Bellini aria, and the camera glides through the old house, showing what it sees, a flight of stairs, a painting on the wall, some small china figurines, clothes laid out on the bed. And from downstairs now you hear the cracking voice of a woman nearing her final days, singing the song of a young woman getting ready for her wedding. The voice sounds like an echo from the beyond. May her life be full of sunshine and love.

Not that the house looks anything like the house in the film, no, it's nothing like, but the atmosphere is the same, a house that's seen its best days, that has only memories, where everything points you to another time, to people who are no longer with us; you can sense things have happened, buried histories, but their traces can no longer be discerned. That's the feeling I mean.

By far the biggest room is the living room, which has a window and a French door opening onto the terrace. Along one wall is a sagging leather sofa, in the middle an old table of dark wood and a couple of chairs. And everywhere, shelves full of books, ordered by authors' names, lots of paperbacks, very little that's new, papers on the table, on the floor, a few pictures on the walls, nothing really remarkable, they look as though they've been there for a hundred years. Outside, a narrow passage leads around two sides of the room to the bathroom, a couple of bedrooms, and the kitchen. The fridge is on, but is empty, apart from a few basics, a bottle of white wine, mineral water, olives, capers, and a half-full jar of sambal oelek. I wish I knew how much sambal oelek is cluttering up the fridges of the world. Has no one ever finished a jar of sambal oelek?

The trash bin has been emptied, which means some kind soul must have been round after Wechsler's death to do the needful, maybe a friend or a neighbor with a key. And then supposed the heirs might have some use for the remaining sambal oelek?

It's obvious that Judith will have Richard's room. I wonder if she'll change the sheets? I don't know the details of his passing, if he died in bed, and at home or in the hospital. They never put that kind of thing in the death announcements, only: after a long illness. And no one thinks to ask. Doesn't matter, I suppose. But the idea of sleeping in sheets in which not long previously a person died—I don't know.

I settle into the room next door, which I suppose was the study and guest room, in the event that Wechsler ever had guests other than Judith. There's a big old desk in it and a queen-size bed. The sheets seem unused, and smell weakly of detergent, Floral Dream or Ocean Breeze, I can't tell, all that stuff smells the same anyway, regardless of the name. Here, too, are lots of shelves, one full of books and magazines, one containing archive boxes, painstakingly labeled cardboard boxes, some of them bearing the names of some of Wechsler's books, others with correspondence, travel records, journalistic work, early writings. That must all be what the archive has its eye on, for some bored and underpaid young Germanist to sift and classify for eternity, or what people take for it.

IT'S TEN by the time we've finished with the washing up. Judith approved of my sauce, but she didn't eat much. We can warm up the leftovers tomorrow. Now Judith is tired and ready for bed.

I'll stay up and read for a bit, you can use the bathroom first.

When I go in there for my shower half an hour later, I can hear her crying through the shut door. I hesitate, stop. Should I knock and try and offer comfort? But what would I say? There, there, not so bad? Of course it's bad for her, and it must have been doubly so as she wasn't able to show it at the funeral. She had to play the minister, offering solace to the relatives, setting life in the context of eternity. And yet her loss is probably the greatest of all. When I come out of the shower, I can't hear her anymore.

Still, I now can't sleep. I scan Wechsler's bookshelves. One row of history and theory of art, one with books on architecture, followed by music, philosophy, religion, and quite a lot on writing and individual writers. All males, all white, and all dead. But hey, he was a dead white man too. No, I'm wrong, there's one on James Baldwin, and one by Natalia Ginzburg on Chekhov, and a life of Natalia Ginzburg by one Maja Pflug. Also books on Annette von Droste-Hülshoff, on Emily Dickinson, Marlen Haushofer, and a life of Johanna Spyri. Sorry, Richard, I did you wrong.

There are a couple of copied pages on the desk. Two lines marked out in red: *un artiste choisit, même quand il se confesse. Et peut-être surtout quand il se confesse. Il allège, il aggrave, ça et là*...Paul Valéry, it says, now who was that again? An artist chooses even when he makes his confession. But what is *alléger*? And what is *aggraver*? Allege and aggravate, or are they false friends? Isn't there a dictionary anywhere? But of course Mr. Wechsler would not have needed one, his French was probably immaculate. No, here's one. To make lighter, to make heavier. The piece is about François Villon, who was that again?

Did Wechsler leave it out for our benefit? He knew the end was coming, it's perfectly possible he reckoned Judith would come, and left her a message. Not to mention the old sambal oelek. Or that he took care to remove things that might have implicated her. Certainly, there are no photographs of Judith anywhere around, but then there are no photos anyway, not in the study, not in the living room.

What would I do if I didn't have much time left to live? Empty out the fridge? Destroy old letters? I read that that's what Johanna Spyri is supposed to have done. Burned all her papers. She's also supposed to have had an affair with Richard Wagner, that's something I'd sooner not think about too much. And to her publisher's suggestion that she write her autobiography, she said the facts of her life weren't interesting, and her inner life was no one's business. That's the way I remember it anyway. Maybe it was completely different, but I've got a lot of time for that woman. Would I write letters to family and friends? By the time you read this, I'll be dead. No, that's too macabre. Just make a quiet exit. I've done enough tidying up in my life, let other people take a turn at it. They can have my money, the stamps in my desk drawer, my extensive collection of foreign coins and all my DVDs by way of recompense. Unfortunately, I've got no sambal oelek. I might perhaps call a person or two, but I wouldn't say anything about my illness, just chat a bit, and try and be extra nice so that they would keep a favorable memory of me.

Wechsler called me in the past year, maybe ten months ago. At eleven at night.

Wechsler: Can you talk?

The question really ought to be: do I feel like talking to the man who ended my career. Well, it hadn't exactly taken off. But I'm a friendly person, and I don't bear grudges, that's just a waste of time. And things come as they are bound to. Perhaps it was even for the best to give up that stubborn dream. At least I'll have a decent pension to look forward to when I retire. And I've completely given up smoking. Almost completely.

Sure. I can talk.

Good.

What's it about?

I'm sorry about the business with the film, he says. But I think I saved us all from wasting a lot of time on a useless endeavor. I should have known it earlier.

So why did you decide to participate in the first place?

Because of you. He pauses for thought. Yes, I think that's right. Pure vanity on my part. It's flattering for an old man to have a young woman interested in him. At least for a while.

Maybe it's the case the other way around too. Perhaps I was flattered by his letting us make the film, trusting us to find out something about him.

Let's skip the thing with the young woman and the old man for now, shall we? We didn't sleep together, after all. And you're not so young as all that, and I'm not so old. And anyway: yawn.

What?

Yawn.

He laughs.

For the record, I find the opponents of gendering are just as obnoxious.

Thanks.

Why is he thanking me? Why is he apologizing? Has he got religion, and is he calling everyone he's wronged in the course of his life? I knew someone like that once. Terrible.

It's a bit like psychotherapy, says Wechsler. You want to believe someone's sitting there who can make sense of it all, the way you never did, but basically you know from the get-go that that's not possible. As soon as you try and explain yourself, you start to fail. So how is anyone else going to…?

I didn't think for a second he called for that, but I don't help him out, he doesn't deserve it. I opened the computer file with our recordings, which I might have deleted long ago, but…we still have some unfinished business. I watch Wechsler walk through Paris. He waits on a street corner, we give him the word, and he sets off like a windup toy. It's humiliating, really.

I'm ill, Wechsler says suddenly, seriously ill. That is, I'm not completely certain. But it seems like I might be.

He tells me the whole story, which now is irrelevant, since illness stories are all about how they end. Isn't that right? Wars end, football games end, do sicknesses end? Never mind. At any rate, he tells me the entire thing and I listen, sometimes I say yes, or oh, or I ask a question when there's something I haven't understood, bile duct? Echogenitation? And he fills me in. Do I have to know those things? Does he?

That's all, really, he says at the end, thank you for listening to me.

I spoke to Judith, I say.

Now he's perplexed.

How did you know...

How did I know what? It wasn't that hard.

Or did I not tell him until the next time he called? Because he called again. First I thought, damn, I'm not the suicide helpline, but then I thought the poor man's got no one else he can talk about it with. Or that he wants to talk about it with. Who do you tell something like that to? Who would I tell it to? Not Tom, for sure. Nor anyone from my family. Most likely someone I hardly knew, but for some reason trusted. A therapist, if you have one, or a minister, maybe. Unless you happen to be having a relationship with one.

That's right, that's what happened: I asked him, Why don't you call Judith. To which he: How did you know...And me: It wasn't that hard.

Judith, he says with a studiedly neutral voice. I heard that voice once before, when we were talking about the sea.

The sea. Period. Judith. Period.

We went for a walk. We had a beer together. More than one. In the bar you used to go to together.

In Winkelried. Did you record her?

No.

He doesn't ask me what I asked Judith, what she told me, what I knew, what I sensed. She didn't tell me anything.

Why don't you talk to her about your illness?

I don't want to alarm her.

Alarm is another of those nice words, even though it doesn't have a nice meaning.

Yes.

When was the last time you spoke to her?

No answer.

When...?

It's better...

What...

Writing.

I am so shit-scared, he says. And then I sometimes feel free and unencumbered. I see the world so differently now, everything is more intense, fear, of course, but joy as well. Whenever I see an old man on the street, an old woman, I think, bonus years. Do you even know what you get with every day? The fact that you're able to get around, drink coffee, go to the shops, walk your dog. When I see children, I think how long they're going to be around for, leading their lives when I'm long dead. What their world will look like, the forest, the town, their houses and apartments, their daily routine. I've never appreciated how beautiful everything is as much as I do now, and I don't want it to end. I want to stay somewhere I've never been.

Is that a quotation? Is he crying?

Are you in pain?

No.

I took notes, I always have a notebook on me, a pad, half journal, half diary, half something. I did it for no particular reason, just out of habit; shit-scared, I wrote down, night sweats, bile duct, echogenitation, Judith. Why do I write these things down? A silence ensues.

We always think the best is yet to come, says Wechsler, as if the whole of bloody life is just a prequel. And then suddenly the shoe drops: There's nothing much to come. That sense of experiencing something for the very last time...

For the very last time, I write down. The last autumn. The last winter. The last spring. Last sex with Judith. Last sausage. Last time I brushed my teeth. And I feel a little sordid, as though I were stealing his emotions.

Perhaps life is like art in that respect, says Wechsler, you can't rehearse either one. You're dropped into it, and then you struggle, or you don't. It's always an emergency.

Emergency, I write down.

I'd like to see the sea again, says Wechsler.

Last time by the sea, I write down.

You should call Judith, I say. She has a right to know.

He laughs very softly. Silence.

Milk, I write. Yogurt, onions, potatoes, lettuce, chicken bouillon, beer. There was something else.

Toilet paper, I say. Damn. But he seems not to have heard anyway.

———

WE TALKED about other things as well. Conversations with a dying man. Is that a good title? Conversations about last things? Would anyone care? Dying isn't terribly original. I still go on writing things down, maybe to bring order into my thoughts.

I found Wechsler more agreeable than before, he wasn't so negative about other writers. Does he like their books any better now? Hardly. But he no longer takes them so personally. For an egomaniac, that's an improvement.

They're just trying to make a living, he says.

Why are people always so aggressive about books they don't like? Instead of simply ignoring them?

Books touch us, says Wechsler, in a way that films and paintings don't. They creep into our brains, mess with our thoughts, stimulate images, give rise to fantasies. That's the good thing about them, but if you think about it, it's also a provocation. And then if we get an author who plays us false, who works with tricks or forces us to see things we don't want in our heads, then it's as though he were operating in our brains against our wishes. Any other kind of artwork you don't care for you can just ignore, but once you've read a book, you're never rid of it. It's like eating spoiled food, you have to vomit it up.

Has he gotten to be more self-critical?

Today I know what I can and can't do. But you mustn't think like that while you're working, otherwise you'll lose your resolve. You mustn't think you're the greatest, you should never think like that, and of course you should always revise and improve everything you've done so far. And every time you make something, you should use all your conviction and determination. Imagine you're standing on a ten-meter board and all the time you're thinking of everything that could go wrong and how you could fail. Then you'll never jump. Or if you do, it'll certainly go wrong. Because you'll lack tautness and poise. So stand at the end, tense your body, count to three, and jump. And then you'll fly.

Strange that he used that example. Did I tell him about the video? Or did he tell me? No, it was Tom. But Tom seems so incredibly far away just now, like someone I was once told about in a story I can barely remember.

Does Tom still exist? Somewhere out there he is leading his life, pursuing his projects, seeing a woman, moving into a new apartment, paying his bills, calling his mother, cooking his three-course meals for himself. It's the opposite of the game we used to play when we were kids: Everyone stops still, you look in their eyes, someone laughs. Then you turn around, and while you're looking away, they run up to you, try and reach you and tag you before you turn around to look again, when they all have to stop still, as though frozen. Tom's stopped. I wonder if I'll ever turn and look in his direction again?

During one of our nighttime phone calls, Wechsler told me his idea for a new religion, a religion not based on faith.

Most people don't believe in anything anyway, and presumably never have. Otherwise they would hardly live the way they do. The founders of religions should have thought about that. So the thing is not to induce people to believe or try to convince them. They should just have said, these are our stories, listen to them and make of them what you will. You can eat whatever you want, you can put on any clothes you like, you can have sex whenever you like with anyone you want. All you have to do is behave reasonably properly, but you do that anyway. Our religion is like a medicine that we prescribe and that makes you immortal. You don't have to understand how it works, you just need to take it three times a day, or once a day, or before or after meals, or once a week, as you please. We have fine words, fine stories, we wear beautiful clothes, we play beautiful music, we burn candles and incense. These are our incantations, our prayers, our rituals. Take them, they won't cost you anything, but they are effective. You don't need to believe us, you will feel the difference. A placebo effect? If you like. But so long as it works.

I laughed. I tried it out, more for the fun of it. I will pray for you, I said. Thank you, he said. And then I did, even while we were still both on the phone. Well, I said, hang on a minute, put down the receiver, and silently said a prayer for him. With hands folded, in the approved manner. Dear God, please make Richard well again and don't let him die.

Did it help? No idea, he died anyway. But it felt good. For him as well. He said so.

Thank you. Again.

HE CALLED every day, every other day. I was kept informed of his condition practically in real time. As though I'd had one of those gizmos you see in hospital dramas that go peep peep peep and show the patient's stats during an operation. And then the peep peep accelerates into a level drone, and everyone goes crazy.

At some point Wechsler stopped calling me. After a couple of days I looked at the notes from our last conversation. Had he said anything about going away, or needing to go into the hospital, or anything like that? I wasn't always paying complete attention while he was talking, because he often went on for hours, until my ear was hot from pressing the receiver against it. Sometimes I distracted myself by doing other stuff at the same time, like ironing or playing computer games. I see hemihepatectomy, I see laparoscopy. I drew little clouds around the terms, and an eye. I like to draw eyes. At school the art teacher showed us how to do them, just one or two little tricks and it looks great. After that, I would draw eyes every chance I got, until someone told me it was a bit weird seeing all those eyes in my textbooks and notebooks, and I stopped. The teachers told us how to do mouths as well. There are just three strokes, a little downturned-sickle shape for the upper lip, a straight line in the middle where the two lips meet, and a slightly longer upturned-sickle shape for the lower lip. Noses are the hardest. The point really is to leave out as much as you can. After all, our faces aren't full of pencil lines, they have shadows. Look, the teacher kept telling us, what was his name again, don't draw what you think you know, draw what you see. A face isn't two eyes, a nose, and a mouth. A face is a whole, a unit, a shape. Ears were hard too.

He was a moody guy, our art teacher, and we were a little afraid of him. I'm sure he would have liked to be an artist himself, he did draw and paint, but on a sort of local level. Maybe he had the odd show in the Basement Gallery, or the Cindy Café, or he designed an overambitious poster for the school nativity play. Perhaps he was a delayed Cubist or something, who knows. I doubt if anyone in the village had ever heard of Cubism. In hindsight, he looks to me like a tragic figure, decent, upright. He never had the least success with his art, but then he never compromised either, he wasn't like one of those canny superstars with their teams and their factories and their merchandising, producing art the way other people make sausages. The ones who pretend they're political and sell their stuff to people who only have money because their grandparents exploited slave labor during the war.

Eliasson, I mean really! Can anyone take him seriously anymore? Love is not enough? No, love is not enough, you need money too. He's produced a cookbook now. Where the dishes are more than just nutrition: they're a source of creative inspiration and communal speech. A lettuce leaf is basically preserved sunlight. When we eat, we receive the world into ourselves and introduce light into our bodies. Vegan light, of course. Risotto of Tuscan kale with mushrooms and rosemary.

And all the other publicity hounds, in twenty or thirty years they'll all be forgotten, but by then they'll have

feathered their nests nicely. My teacher wasn't like that—
moody, irascible, passionate, empathetic, presumably an
alcoholic. I'm sure Eliasson goes jogging and cooks himself three-course vegan meals.

Maybe my teacher was the reason I applied to art
school. One time he said to me, It's not a question of making, it's about finding. That may have been the most important thing anyone ever said to me in my whole career.
So-called. Maybe I'm a bit of a sad case too. I should really go back to making films again. Or write a book. But
what about? You shouldn't write a book *about* anything,
I remember Wechsler saying once, or not a novel anyway.

Small intestine loop, it says in my notebook. And
what's that next to it? Is that the small intestine? It looks
like an earthworm.

NEXT TO the desk I find an open archive box. The label
reads A Fantasy in Time. I take out the contents, a stack of
paper, a leaflet on the Chapelle de l'Epiphanie that Richard led us to back then, an information pack on the Missions Etrangères, a brochure for the hotel in his village
where we had been going to meet. A card: Welcome! A
warm welcome to our team. We look forward to working
with you, and hope you have a fantastic start. There are
a couple of pages of newspaper clippings too, some sentences highlighted, an article from *The New Yorker*, "Making Sense of Who We Might Have Been," that doesn't give
much away, but ends with a beautiful sentence: Much must

be left unsaid, unseen, unlived. Also in the pile are a few printouts of poems, Eichendorff, "On the Death of My Child," Thomas Brasch, Dylan Thomas, Andreas Gryphius, a fairly incomplete and contradictory timetable, photos from our film shoot in Paris, I really don't know how he made them, and finally a small notebook.

The entries begin more or less at the time we started talking together about our film idea, the first one goes: The conquest of time. Moving consciously in time, first cautiously, then more and more boldly.

They seem to be notes toward a novel that Richard never completed. Characters are named by initials only, W. and A. being the most common, but also J. and T. and sometimes a daughter for W. While I read the notes, I can see the book before me not as a book but as a kind of space in which I move, a twisting structure of thoughts, where I make my discoveries:

His house in Paris, as though he'd never lived in it: just books, many, many books. Perhaps he doesn't live in the house at all, or it's just a possible life he could have lived.

W. has lived nowhere, does he actually exist? All trace of him is lost in uncertainty.

W. and A. picture the village. A. lives with him in his house. Who writes the book?

Perhaps W. dies.

It's the most exciting thing about literature. Making things up. Ágota Kristóf.

A: He's watching us.

W. has a daughter, who lives in the village.

When A. has a thought, W. seems able to sense it, but how?

Nothing fits together.

High-altitude fog.

The art of permitting chance without losing sight of form. Chance therefore as an element of form. But how do you dominate it?

A. finds a notebook of W.'s.

I look up in consternation, as though I'd been caught red-handed, but I'm all alone in the room. The next item is a shopping list:

Milk

Yogurt

Onions

Potatoes

Lettuce

Chicken bouillon

Beer

Toilet paper

And then more notes for the book.

A: Would you have had a different life if you hadn't written?

A dog (pug) licks a man's shaved legs.

A. walks into W.'s house and finds it empty.

W.: I am increasingly self-sufficient.

Perhaps W. does not exist?

What does it mean when the author dies? Is it like God is dead?

Is the truth important? What actually happened?

Any event in any of our lives transforms everything that happened previously.

W.: Withdrawing from the film was his only way of saving himself.

All the nonsense I speak every day, all the attempts to grasp something. Thinking in circles.

A thought, an action.

To see the sea for the last time.

To see the sea as though for the first time. But how? Will I finally be able to say any more than that the surf crashes? Jürgen Hosemann, *The Sea on 31 August.*

The secret of redemption is memory.

Is it acceptable to offer condolences on the death of a dog?

Surfaces of water in a section of land, next to a harvested pumpkin field, with a few unripe, wretched-looking pumpkins in the ragged-looking foliage. A meadow with apple orchard. From the road, an avenue of trees leads up to the ponds, birches, some newly planted, others veterans with boils on their trunks. Nesting boxes are hanging on the trees.

If, following my death, you want to write my biography, nothing could be easier than that. There are two dates—the date of my birth and the date of my death. All the days in between are mine. Alberto Caeiro, aka Fernando Pessoa, the Keeper of Sheep.

It's not the author who narrates, it's the people and the facts who do.

I am at home in my texts.

Silence.

I wonder what sort of book it would have made? Was A. a reference to me, and J. to Judith? But didn't he say once that he never wrote about real people, that his characters were always invented? What if Judith and I were inventions?

I think I must have had too much wine. Time to hit the sack.

WHEN I get up in the morning, Judith has already been out to get baguettes and croissants and made coffee. After breakfast, we sit in the living room, me with my laptop on my lap, Judith with one of Richard's books. She seems not to want to poke around in his things. Not because of the heirs, because of him. It does seem a bit transgressive, you'd have to say. And she doesn't know what she'll find. Maybe there were other women in his life, I'm sure there were. She had another man in hers, after all, so she can hardly expect him to revere her the way a monk reveres the Virgin Mary and lead a chaste life. But the comparison's a bit off. They did after all sleep together, even if they never saw that much of each other. Pretty unchaste, if you ask me. Although she hasn't told me any of the details. All she said was that she had a love affair with Richard. That was her word, for liaison or relationship or romance. It was a bit strange to hear her say it like that. It was dark up on the mountainside, and as I say, I had the sense she was talking to herself. But for a minister, who just moments earlier you were talking about altarpieces with, suddenly to start telling you things about her private life, that is a bit weird. Richard is the love of my life, and I am the love of his life, she said it with the utmost conviction and certainty. Almost aggressively. It seemed to have something liberating in it for her. She must have kept it locked up inside of herself for all those years, her guilty conscience, and also her joy in the relationship, her surprise at herself, and even a kind of pride, that she, the minister of the locality, who to everyone seemed so sensible, so calm, so Protestant, even, let's face it, so boring, that this minister had another side to her. A dark side. Or if you prefer, a lighter side. That was probably what she was wanting to tell me.

At any rate, that day we went out into the park, which is just a hundred yards away from the house. It looked a bit the way I imagine Versailles, only without the actual Versailles. No palace, then. But enormous! With a great long ornamental pond and avenues of trees, hedges, flower beds, lawns, and woods; on a slope there were a series of fountains dropping from pool to pool; there were springs, statues, an orangery, a café, playgrounds; in one corner a soccer field and tennis courts. The whole thing had to be a kilometer square.

We ambled around that park for what must have been a couple of hours, just talking. The morning clientele was composed of joggers and dogwalkers, and a couple of ladies in charge of a gang of children wearing Day-Glo vests and running around squawking like a flock of sparrows.

Although it might be objected that sparrows fly more than they run.

This is something that has preoccupied me for a while now, I don't know why it's sprung to mind now, perhaps it's seeing so many people with their dogs: Is it right to offer condolences on the death of a dog? Or is that somehow impious? Should you just say, I'm sorry for your loss, but it was just a dog?

Judith laughs. Of course it's all right. Condolence means nothing more or less than to suffer with, *con-*, with, *dolere*, to suffer or grieve. Whenever anyone suffers, you can suffer along with them.

Perhaps I should have taken Latin in school after all. Two women come toward us with a baby carriage, and one of them has a cat on a leash. A cat!

And cats?

You can mourn the death of a cat as well, says Judith.

And what if a car breaks down? Or a washing machine?

Well, says Judith, I might draw the line there.

We walked along splendid avenues of trees, long symmetrical rows of trimmed trees; behind them is forest with a tangle of paths and walkways, undergrowth and dead twigs.

Look, Judith laughs and points me discreetly to a bench where a man is sitting in shorts, with a pug sitting at his feet, licking his legs.

Did you ever read *All the Days of My Life*? Judith asks.

I don't think so.

That was his fourth or fifth title.

It sounds a bit kitschy.

One thing have I desired of the LORD, that will I seek after; that I may dwell in the house of the LORD all the days of my life, to behold the beauty of the LORD, and to inquire in his temple.

Psalm 27, says Judith, but it's not really relevant to the book.

Do you know the Bible by heart?

No, she says, laughing again. Don't tell anyone. Just a few especially important or beautiful passages.

I always forget the titles of books I've read, and often the names of the characters and the plot, and always the name of whoever wrote it.

So what's left for you to remember?

The book, I say, feeling rather stupid.

JUDITH TELLS me a story. It's about a Swiss teacher living in Paris. He lives quietly, has occasional love affairs, does his work more from habit than pleasure, and one day he gets sick. Or he thinks he's sick, he has symptoms. And then from one day to the next, his life is turned upside down, he ends his affairs, leaves his friends, sells his apartment, resigns from his job, and returns to Switzerland, to the village where he grew up, to see his first love once again. She has gotten married in the meantime, but agrees to see him anyway. They meet at a small lake where they used to go swimming decades ago, where they once kissed. And then it happens: they make love by the side of the lake.

It's our story, says Judith. Except that he wasn't sick. At least not then.

It's all there: the village, the water, the woman.

We were by the lake.

I tell Judith about our side trip on our way up to the village. She says, wrong lake, they had never gone there, it was far too far away.

But Richard had given me the name of the lake. Had he done it to dupe us, or did the fiction already seem more real than the reality? I'm not the woman, and the man isn't Richard, and it wasn't by the lake, it was in the Auenwald woods, says Judith, but the book tells our story.

That plot seems familiar to me, and I think I must have read the novel, though I have a completely different memory of it. There was another, younger woman, whom the man took with him back to the village, with whom he was having an affair. I remember being annoyed about that. Why does he take his mistress with him when he wants to hook up with his first love? Just in case? If Plan A fails? Then he sends her packing, it's a pretty ugly, heartless scene, at the station as I remember. He wants to give her money for the train ticket, the asshole, and she says something like: Are you crazy. Judith seems to have completely erased that woman. And then the first love does sleep with him, but she says that's just a story, and not the reality. The reality is her husband and children and that she had to go to make lunch for them. So you see, I did remember some of it after all.

I reread those parts in the afternoon. After all, there's no shortage of Richard's books in the house. In fact, it's a really sad story. The man imagines what might have been if he'd got together with the woman. He knows they don't really fit, and they were far too young at the time, and he imagines how unhappy he could have made her. And then he thinks the only reason his feeling for her lasted as long as it did was because it was never fulfilled. All this is at their final meeting, in a little house in the woods. He asks her, What are you thinking about, and she says, Oh, nothing. Of course I read it, in fact I think it was my favorite of his.

But for Judith it seems to be a completely different book, the overture to her story, which while it may not have had a happy ending, was at least happier than that.

In the café next to the little château, we split a mediocre sandwich and trooped off home.

Judith wants a bit of a rest. She goes into Wechsler's room, but leaves the door open a crack, as though not to sever communications with me, and not to be completely alone with the ghost of her lover. I lie down on the bed in the office or spare room, look for the passages in the book, and then start reading again from the beginning. When I read Wechsler's books, I always have the feeling I'm hearing the voices of the dead, I don't know why. It has something consoling, a sense that they're still around, even though they're long dead. I don't even need to read the books, it's enough to just look at them to start remembering.

I could help myself to a book here, there are enough copies around, and they would only wind up in the recycling otherwise. Save Richard's work, so that his voice isn't extinguished.

To Judith, I must seem like a kind of Cerberus, guarding Richard's papers: if she wants to get at anything, she has to get past me. Google: Cerberus, aka Kerberos, or Demon of the Dark. In Greek mythology, the many-headed dog who guarded the entrance to the underworld and so prevented the escape of the shades. So the shades need watching too? It's possible to bribe him with honey cake. That's what they had in the South of France, those gluey squares in plastic wrap, soft, sticky stuff with some kind of spice in them, a bit like gingerbread, I didn't care for them. I don't like gingerbread either. I'm not really one for sweet things in general. Does anyone care?

WHEN I hear Judith getting up, I move to the living room to clear the way for her. I'm not a demon of the dark, not my sister's keeper. I don't want to be a many-headed Cerberus or Kerberos, much less do I want to be fed honey cake. What business is it of mine?

This was wild: when we were walking up the mountain, Judith showed me something on her mobile. She always deleted his emails right away, she said. Where did I read that women are much better at concealing their affairs than men? Anyway, she would delete them immediately after reading them. Also the pictures he sent her. Glimpsed them, committed them to memory, and wiped them.

But sometimes I copied and saved the odd sentence from his messages, she said.

She showed me the document in question, a string of sentences that made no pretense at coherence:

In my heart of hearts you've been my lover for a very long time. Because we belong together. With the most beautiful woman in the world. Everything about you is beautiful, my darling. I love you, I can't help it. There's nothing about you I would change. You have bewitched me. Your love is so beautiful. Kind Fate. Let me say again how much I love you. Your hills and hollows. I think you were up for it from the very beginning, perhaps without even knowing it. We belong together.

It's strange, slightly mad, but lovely.

Dinner in the Japanese restaurant. We are the only diners. The food is good, but the portions are tiny. Therefore: four stars.

THE MAN I met at the Gare de Lyon wants to meet me. The one with the woman who was blowing him kisses. We exchanged a few emails, fairly earthy stuff. For some reason, I let him know I was visiting Paris. And now he wants to see me. Well, probably more than just see me. As luck would have it, the kiss-blower is back in Lyons, where her company... well, anyway, she's not around. And he could manage some time in the day. He works from home mainly, I forget what it is he does. Or if you prefer: it never interested me. One of those jobs that prompts the question, how did mankind ever get by for thousands of years without them? Communications adviser, marketing specialist, compliance officer, Lord knows. But it comes with the kind of salary that runs to designer furniture and holidays in Southeast Asia. I once heard one woman saying to another in the streetcar, you know, if you have a stereo system like ours, children are out of the question. Crazy Romans.

I have something I need to do in the city. An appointment to see someone.

Judith doesn't ask. Maybe she's happy to get some time in the house on her own. Then she can sift through things in quiet, maybe make the odd item disappear. Is she worried in case Richard's sister betrays her? I don't know her, strangely we didn't even hear of her existence, otherwise we would have tried to interview her. Then she could have told us: My brother always had a rich imagination, even as a child he liked to write, we quarreled all the time, but we were the best of friends, just the usual rubbish you get in these situations. If I were to ever get wind of someone having an affair with someone not her husband (and not mine either!), then I definitely wouldn't give her away.

So I meet Marc for lunch. He has a rather tiresomely formal manner, as though we didn't both know where this was going, as though we hadn't exchanged those emails. Is that a French thing? Keeping up appearances? He recommends the tuna with arugula, but in the first place I don't like arugula, and then I don't like tuna, and third it's wrong to eat it anyway, either on account of the dolphins, or because the stocks are overfished or for some other reason I can't remember. I order a goat cheese salad. Then, as I'm eating it, I start to wonder if you can smell it on your breath. Never mind, Marc is young and impetuous, maybe a little starved as well, that has advantages. Admittedly, some disadvantages too. At any rate, I bet the smell of goat cheese isn't enough to put him off.

The afternoon passes to my entire satisfaction. Afterward we go for a little drink and sit facing one another, without much to say. Marc tries to tell me something about his work, but he can surely tell that that's about my least-favorite subject in the world. We have nothing to say to one another, as I now see. We're all excitement beforehand, all disillusionment afterward. A second glass of chardonnay doesn't help either, in fact I feel really wretched.

Ciao.

We probably both sense we won't be seeing each other again. And we won't write each other either. At least that's one thing I've accomplished with my day.

I HAVE a bad conscience on my way back to Sceaux. I feel as though I've gone behind Judith's back and deceived Richard, even though I'm under no obligation to him and there was never anything between us. But we're here on account of him, and to think about him, to remember him, and now everything just feels sad and the mood is gone, the melancholy, autumnal feeling, the connection with Richard beyond the tomb. The spell is broken, I am expelled from the society of mourning women, I have been found unworthy of thinking about Richard Wechsler.

I spend a long time traipsing around the area, not because I can't find the house, but because I'm trying to recover my state of mind before my excursion, the state I was in when I told Judith at the funeral that it wasn't sad, and believed it. And then it's all over, and we're standing there together on a sunny day in September, thinking about him a little bit, and afterward we just go home. But this time I hadn't gone home, I was with Marc. The bed is from Switzerland as well, Marc says, it's by a firm called Lehni. Well, congratulations. Monsieur likes to repose on superior-quality Swiss craftsmanship. Wechsler would presumably understand that, and either approve of it or think it was amusing, but the thought bothers me, not for moral reasons but aesthetic ones.

I walk around the hushed precinct, along the concentric streets, look into the gardens that are as deserted as the streets, as the houses appear to be. Has something happened to all the people who live here? There was a book about someone who one morning wakes up, and all the other people are gone. Were they all dead, and no one besides him left on the planet? And as there was no one left on earth, he wanted to go to heaven, but the moon was a piece of rotten wood... I know my classics. And then there was another book by an Austrian, and one children's book I think was called *The Green Cloud*. And when it wanted to return to Earth, the Earth was an upset harbor, and it sat down and wept, and it's still sitting there, all alone. That's how I seem to myself.

IT'S GETTING dark. The park will be locked in half an hour. Fifty yards inside the gate there is a little playground with a few benches, there I sit in my harbor. There is nothing sadder than a deserted playground. The promise of a better life full of swings and seesaws and merry-go-rounds that always proves false. Free time is such a sorry affair anyway. The mere word. Free time, freedom. What does a person do in complete freedom? He swings, he turns in circles, he rocks up and down till he's completely giddy. Or worse: he gives himself a treat. Tom was capable of cooking a three-course dinner for himself. When someone canceled a meeting, and I unexpectedly turned up at home, he had set the table for himself as in a restaurant, with two plates for first course and entrée, cloth napkin, water and wineglasses and the appropriate silverware. He had even lit himself a candle. Wonder why it made me so incensed? Really, I should have admired him, but for some reason it made me angry, as though I'd caught him watching porn films. I always felt best when I was working, and the more wretched the sandwich I bought myself, the better I liked it. If I had a therapist, I think I would talk to him about that. Just as well I don't.

There is no one in the park, not even joggers. I'm the last. I sit on one of the benches by the playground and have a little cry, that does me good. After that, I'm ready to go back to Judith, even as a park attendant walks up and shoos me away.

On ferme.

There, that would be a job, park attendant. Or cemetery gardener, super in a public building. Postman. You're out in the fresh air all day, get exercise, meet people, and

spread a little happiness wherever you go ringing door-
bells. When I was little, our postman made a habit of
reading all our postcards, and then he would say: Oh, so
the children are away skiing, are they? Or: I'm glad your
grandmother's doing better. He took part in the life of the
whole area, and didn't see anything wrong with breaching
the confidentiality of the mail. I think everyone back then
accepted it, just as we accepted other things as well. Thou
shalt not muzzle the mouth of the ox that treadeth out the
corn, it says in Scripture.

The house is dark, but the door isn't locked. I walk in,
turn on a light, and switch it off again. I look in the office,
which is in the gloaming, nothing seems to have shifted
there. Judith is on the bed in Richard's bedroom, asleep.
She's lying on her back like a dead person and looks beautiful, more relaxed than I've ever seen her. Perhaps she's
dreaming of Richard and their meetings in Paris. I gaze at
her body and picture her making love with Richard, both
very close and very separate.

I am Richard, eyeing Judith. I see the girl she once
was, the girl I first fell in love with. Judith, I say the name
tonelessly, Judith.

In one of our telephone calls, Wechsler tells me
about their first meeting. It was before they went to high
school, a weekend trip with an evangelical youth organization. It didn't have much to do with religion, mind
you, said Wechsler, it was just a chance to get out of the
village without having to be too sporty. We went up into
the hills, I don't remember exactly where, but I think it

was the pre-Alps, perhaps Toggenburg. I remember lying around a campfire in a meadow. We had blankets, and talked about everything under the sun. I had never noticed Judith before, she was quiet, not shy, but demure, perhaps because she was the minister's daughter. But that kind of thing didn't matter in our group, we were all the children of someone or other. How old would we have been at the time? Fifteen? Sixteen? I don't know. Was there a minister or youth worker around, chaperoning? Bound to have been. But not at the campfire. Someone playing the guitar? Certainly. It got cold, the dew fell on the meadow and on us in our blankets. We talked more softly, only two of us now. Me and Judith. Have you noticed the change in acoustics when the sun goes down? The air seems to turn thinner and more transparent, space opens. We talked about our plans for the future. Did Judith already want to study theology? Was I already set on writing? I was an atheist, I was of the age where you think you know everything and you understand nothing. That was the beginning.

Judith had told me how it developed. Many years, half a lifetime in which they continually approached and left one another. Sometimes she would hear nothing from Richard for the longest time, then suddenly he was back, writing one email after another, wanting to see her, only to disappear again afterward. I never really knew where he was or what he was up to, he was like a ghost, albeit a friendly ghost. He sent me all his books with cryptic dedications. Sometimes I wished he would get out of my life and leave me in peace, maybe because I sensed he could become dangerous to me.

And was he dangerous to you?

Do you know the Udo Lindenberg song "Bullet in Your Colt," asked Judith.

God, is he still alive?!

Richard taped it for me. Do you remember cassette tapes? I think that was the moment I first understood he was in love with me. I'd probably guessed it for a long time, but that was when I knew it. What it signified, what it signified for me.

I am the bullet in your Colt
Shoot me straight into your heart
Or shoot me right out of your life
I need to know what's going on
After the shot there's no more questions
And you'll know I'm all yours.

Judith sang two or three lines of it to me in her surprisingly fine voice. Then she laughed, a warm, sincere laugh. He was always a terribly sentimental character. Usually he was able to keep it out of sight. I was still at college then, and already with my present husband. Of course there was no possibility of getting into anything with Richard. But it was the first little scratch on the smooth veneer of my project, a little crack that deepened as I got older. I fought it for a long time, said Judith. But in the end there were no more questions.

I am Richard. I sit down on the side of the bed and contemplate this woman who to me has not grown old, and I am astonished by her and by myself, by the love that has connected us over all these years and never brought us together. I can't help but reach out and touch Judith, I brush the hair back from her brow, put my hand on her shoulder, graze her neck. I am almost alarmed by the heat of her body. Finally, she wakes, looks at me, smiles, and says nothing.

Over supper, I tell Judith about my phone calls with Richard. She listens, seemingly unmoved, neither angry with me nor disappointed. Was I expecting that reaction? Was I perhaps only telling her to make myself important? To say to her, listen, when things were critical, it was me he called, not you. Am I jealous of the strange love story between her and Richard? I don't think so. I like Judith, and from my perspective she's welcome to everything she experienced with him. Does that sound disingenuous? I think it does, even though I don't mean it to. Can you be disingenuous without knowing it or meaning it? Perhaps I'm a kind of parasite who sucks up her love to feed myself on it. One of those plants that only flourishes on other plants. Like mistletoe. If people pass underneath me, they have to kiss.

I tell Judith about one of our last conversations. Richard seemed to be doing well that day. I don't mean physically, I don't know the first thing about that. But in a good mood.

I can't say I'm reconciled to it, he says, but I at least accept it. I've had a good life, and a long one. When I think of all the writers who died much younger, Büchner, Kleist, Kafka, Pessoa, Chekhov, Camus, Pavese...

Suicides don't count. They're to blame for what happened.

But even without them. Borchert. Even W. G. Sebald.

Why even? And what about women?

They have longer lives. He laughed. No quotas for mortality.

Annette von Droste-Hülshoff, Ingeborg Bachmann, Marlen Haushofer, Emily Dickinson, Sylvia Plath...

There you go again. Suicide!

Smarty-pants.

This whole dying business bores me, he said. If I don't have much longer to live, then I don't want to spend my last days relaying status reports on my innards. Or writing a book: *Die Happy with Richard Wechsler*, instructions for beginners and advanced students. Let's talk about books.

Are you writing?

I've written enough.

Last words?

If I had to die now, I'd say: Was that it? And: I didn't really understand it. And: It was a bit noisy.

Is that yours?

No, it's Tucholsky. Another suicide.

Karl Valentin is supposed to have said, I didn't know dying was so beautiful.

That's a matter of opinion. Do you know "The Dumpling Song"?

Damn, wrong cue. Now he starts telling me Karl Valentin and Liesl Karlstadt gags in a horrible faux-Bavarian
accent. As though I hadn't heard them all before. I used to
love them when I was little. He did a terrible job, only half
remembers them, messed up the endings where there were
any endings to mess up. He didn't have the patience for the
endless repetitions that Valentin's jokes require, that whole
not-being-able-to-stop. Ironic, when you think he'd told me
himself—this must have been in Paris—he could never stop,
was no good at ending friendships, ending relationships, he
had never been able to give anything up to start afresh. I've
lived the same life for decades, living in the same house,
eating in the same restaurants, meeting the same people,
wearing the same clothes, using the same products.

And what about your books? Do you find them hard
to end?

He hesitated briefly, and then, as though he'd never
given it any thought before, No, it's the easiest thing. The
endings seem to write themselves.

He was still doing his Karl Valentin impressions. *The
Confirmand*. And so I say it once again, youth is a lovely
time, you only get it once.

That's enough of that! I know them all, and it's not
possible to imitate them.

Tell me a single scene from your film that's anything
more than an illustration. Where the image does something you can't convey in words.

Why is he back on the film now? Was he trying to
annoy me? Or did he have a bad conscience about it? So

now he wanted it confirmed to him that no good result would have come from it? I'm damned if I'm going to help with that.

There were a couple of nice things we could have shot in the village.

Like cats in the rain, you mean?

Touché! But how did he know?

All that endless traipsing around in the city, he said, that was just filler. You might as well have had footage of kittens playing with balls of wool while I was trying to articulate my deepest insights into the nature of literature and the order of the world. Or Caribbean sunsets, the wonders of the oceans, slow-motion reels of girl gymnasts.

Half of a film gets made in the cutting room.

You get nothing from nothing.

Thanks.

Pleasure.

But I was glad he was feeling better. After that, we didn't speak about his illness anymore.

IT WASN'T until we cleared the table that I notice the stack of letters on it, maybe forty or fifty envelopes. Some of them still have that pretty red-and-blue airmail striping around the edge, and are written on that very thin, almost transparent, blue paper. Judith doesn't comment, but she doesn't remove the letters either. She could easily have stuffed them into her suitcase or thrown them away. Before long, she excuses herself, saying she's tired. The woman seems to need constant rest. Is that what awaits when you're pushing sixty? Or is it that she finds the situation so emotionally exhausting?

The stack of letters sits on the table in mute challenge. I sit on the sofa, still reading the book of Richard's we were talking about yesterday. And there, almost at the end, I find the little passage we had been going to put at the beginning of our film: He asked himself how much time they would have left. But all that didn't matter. The future was just one day.

They are Judith's letters, his are lost for all time, she destroyed them, and he doesn't seem to have kept any copies, not like those authors writing to their mistresses and already thinking of posterity. See what kind of a man I was. He never seemed that calculating, that vain, to me. Posterity doesn't exist, he said once. The future is just one day.

Dear Richard, Beloved Richard, My Beloved, My Darling... I push the letters away. Not out of discretion, out of forbearance. Reading them wouldn't do anything, they don't interest me. No more than reading recipes I will never make. A pure waste of time. Risotto of Tuscan kale with mushrooms and rosemary. They were lovers, but their letters are in a code I don't understand. Or understand all too well. I don't want to hear about Judith's desire, her hunger, her lust. Been there, done that, got the T-shirt.

Question: Why does Judith want me to read them? Does she want a witness? The way a couple needs witnesses for a wedding? Beloved friends, we are gathered together to celebrate the extramarital relationship of Judith and Richard. They first met when they were little more than children, but it took many years for their friendship to take its current form. Judith was married to the amateur photographer, little if anything is known about the emotional life of Richard. All we know is that on the occasion of a funeral and presumably with drink taken, they decided to take this one further step, which they accomplished that same day, and which today we are gathered to affirm. Do you, Judith Imbach, hereby take Richard Wechsler for your lover, to love and honor and conduct a liaison with on good days as on bad, until death do you part, then say, yes, so help me God. Well, I suppose one could do that without God's help.

And Judith: Yes, I do.

And Richard...I do.

You may kiss.

Now I know what this is about. Judith wants me to read her letters because she doesn't want to read them herself. This morning I woke up early and stayed in bed. I love the blue twilight hour between night and day, this drowsy state halfway between sleeping and waking. From outside I hear an occasional car, and from somewhere inside there's a hum, which could be the fridge, and a click and a whoosh that might be the boiler, then there's birds in the garden and from far away a sort of all-purpose soughing that might be the sound of time.

Suddenly I knew it: Judith won't read the letters. She'll throw them away today or tomorrow. She won't burn them or rip them up, she will in her undramatic way drop them in the bin and leave the bin bag in the container by the side of the road when we go. Game over. End of story.

AS FAR as I was concerned, we could have stayed in Richard's house forever. Time seemed to stand still, and since Richard's death, time here literally had stopped. One day, someone with a purpose will walk in, and then all the passed time will come flooding into the house and wash away the stopped time and everything else. And then it will no longer be Richard's house, just an abandoned residence full of junk needing to be cleared, valued, demolished, renovated, or sold to someone who will want to lead a completely new life in it.

But for now Richard is still present everywhere, in his clothes, his books, his furniture and the pictures on the walls, in his kitchen and garden equipment, his old bicycle, in the collapsible chairs on the terrace and the deck chair, in all the junk acquired over the course of a lifetime. Maybe most of all in the little things, an opened bar of white chocolate in the cupboard, a bent paper clip, wonder what he used that for, an opened letter from the utilities company where he's ringed a couple of places, probably trying out a new pen, an opened box of Band-Aids, and beside it the white strip of waxed paper peeled off the adhesive surface, perhaps he cut himself shaving not long before his death? Richard won't be back, won't contribute any new things or remove any old ones, won't use anything or change anything. He hangs over the house and the garden like a ghost, like a thought, like a memory.

If only there were a work possible that was formulated outside our own being, a work that would allow us to step outside the limitations of our individual I, to give speech to things that have no speech, the bird in the gutter, the tree in spring and the same tree in fall, the stone, the cement, the plastic coating…

I'm sure that was another one of his quotes, Richard didn't improvise such things, even if he didn't complete the sentence.

We ought to set up the Richard Wechsler Museum here, and just leave everything exactly as it is. Then we wouldn't let anyone in, just put a sign up outside, Richard Wechsler Museum, permanently closed.

Then the two of us would be the museum curators, and put on different exhibits, says Judith. Richard Wechsler's collection of holey socks.

Sambal oelek and other items from Richard Wechsler's pantry. Literary-culinary investigations.

We could display the five packets of spaghetti that are in the kitchen cupboard.

Uncompleted projects, unpaid bills.

Empty notebooks, full bookshelves. Speech and speechlessness in the life and work of Richard Wechsler.

You would man the till and I would be in charge of security, says Judith. Then at the end of the week, we'd swap jobs.

But Judith has to go back. All sorts of things are waiting for her, a seminar, Aging Ahoy, an autumn peregrina-
tion with confirmands, and the Harvest Festival, followed
by cake.

What will you talk about?

The feeding of the four thousand.

Isn't that one of the miracles?

Yes, that's right, the one with the loaves and fishes.

And what is there to say about it? Beyond just tuck in?

Oh, this and that, groans Judith. About bread alone
not satisfying us and Jesus as the staff of life and on sharing, solidarity, poverty, refugees, all that. It's all so shallow.
Do you remember how you asked me if you had to have
faith to work as a minister?

You said you didn't have to, but it helped if you did.

Yes, says Judith, it would help. Especially now.

She says her faith had always been unquestioning, she
had taken it in with her mother's milk, the Bible stories
and evening prayers, the Sunday services and holy days,
the singing, the nice clothes she had to wear, her father,
who must not be disturbed when he was composing his
sermon, all that had been part of her belief. Then, when
she started studying, matters had become more serious
and consequential. We studied and compared the sources,
did textual analysis, questioned the rudiments of faith. I
lost my naive children's faith, which was replaced by something new, pleasure in the old writings, the complexity of
the interpretations, hermeneutics, philosophy, mysticism.
I read the old books and had the feeling no one had ever

read them before me, everything suddenly clicked and meant something to me. Then I went out into the world, and things were different again, then it was the application of faith, I could help people, reassure them when they were assailed by doubt, comfort them in their sorrow, suggest where they might find answers, or at the very least find their own questions put by others before them. I had the feeling I was doing important work, even if I often came up against my own limits and doubted my own convictions. But people believed in me, and so I came to believe them and in my own vocation. Then the thing with Richard began, but even that I was able to file away somehow. No one is without fault, he that is without sin among you, throw the first stone. Even my reluctance to end things with Richard was something I could process. I never felt it to be adultery, even if in the eyes of society it was just that. There were far worse sins in my system of values. Pride, arrogance, envy, lack of love. Of course. Perhaps my sin was my last chance not to lose my faith. My bad conscience was proof that not everything was a matter of indifference to me. But then Richard died...

For the first time, she breaks down in front of me. I hold her in my arms, stroke her head. To begin with, she was crying just a little, then she started sobbing, and then for some stupid reason, I start to cry too, I have no idea why.

When was it he said he wanted his books and nothing else of his to endure? No diaries, no letters, no photographs, no obituaries, no stories people exchange about him, not even a stone.

What about your family? Your loved ones?

I could tell that he hadn't thought about them. Typical. He preferred not to give me an answer.

WHY IS it that the French can't manage to announce a departure track ahead of time? In Germany and Switzerland and even in Austria, a train always leaves from the same track, it's displayed on the printed timetable a year in advance, and if there's ever any irregularity, there are a dozen PA announcements and a groveling apology from the stationmaster. In France the passengers are left cluelessly milling around in the departure hall, and then five minutes before the scheduled departure, the identity of the track is finally revealed, and the entire mob makes its way there, pushing and shoving, and in the end the train is delayed because people haven't managed to get on in time. Why do I get annoyed about trivial things like that?

Which is worse, to lose your lover or your faith? There was a story once about a Buddhist monk that I remember from when I was a teenager. The local primary school had organized a series of talks on world religions, and I went to all of them. Was I on some kind of quest? Still hoping for answers? Anyway, this story about a Buddhist monk and his little dog stayed with me. The monk was readying himself to go into the state of nirvana or whatever it's called, and he didn't want to leave his little dog behind. That turned out to be the last test in an examination he thereby passed. What happened then I can't remember.

Did he and his dog reach nirvana together? In my recollec-
tion, they moved on, an old man in robe and sandals and
his dog on a dusty road in mountainous terrain. The camera stops, and the two of them walk on, becoming smaller
and smaller until they finally disappear over a line of hills
on the horizon. Cut.

Did Judith discard the letters? When I went into the
kitchen the following morning, they were gone. I didn't say
anything, didn't ask any questions, didn't even look in the
bin. We packed our bags, removed traces of our having
been there, and took the suburban line into the city, to the
Gare de Lyon, where we caught the train home.

Judith is very quiet. She has pulled out her book on
Jewish mysticism again, turned over some pages, read a
little bit, but then shut it after a few minutes. Now it's
lying on her lap, she has a finger in the place she's got to,
and she's looking out the window. Does the scene outside
mean anything to her, or is it just emptiness filling her?
A body moves through space. Is that our salvation, our
consolation? Being between places? My exuberance when
I ran off with Richard. We only went as far as the nearest
café, but if he'd asked me then, I would have gone with
him to the ends of the earth. Or at least to his house in the
suburbs. I wasn't in love with him or anything, it was just
euphoria, abdication, pleasure in movement. That to me is
the worst aspect of death, nothing moves anymore.

I am unable to read anything in Judith's features. Is
she happy to have accomplished her mission? Is she sad?
Would she rather have stayed in Paris? Is she dreading the

return to her village? Is she thinking of Richard—or of her husband? The rest of her life? Or the miraculous feeding of the four thousand?

Look, she suddenly says, opening her book as though to read me something from it. Then from memory she quotes from Baal Shem Tov: Not forgetfulness! The secret of redemption is memory.

Silence. After a while she asks me: Do you think that's true?

What is redemption? Do you want to be redeemed?

Judith shrugs her shoulders. I don't know anymore.

Do you want to look at the footage we took of him in Paris?

She nods, and I scoot around next to her, open up my laptop, and start the video I cut together back in the hotel in the village. I realize I've shown it to Judith once already, on our first evening together. Never mind now. Full screen.

Richard, walking in the cemetery at Montparnasse, stops in front of the grave of Suzanne and Samuel Beckett. No quotation on the polished-granite slab, no last words, no big production, just the names and dates. A bunch of yellow asters in clear wrapping is left lying on the stone. Richard stops a moment, scratches his head, and moves on. Cut. He is walking along the Boulevard Raspail, cut, through the Jardin du Luxembourg, cut, down the Boulevard Saint-Michel. A green garbage truck comes into shot, garbagemen tip the contents of large containers into the maw at the back. Richard walks on. Cut. He walks down a narrow alleyway, restaurants, a bakery, a bookstore. Cut. Now we're down by the Seine, he looks at the displays in the secondhand book stalls. Did we tell him to do that? Buy something, or at least make a pretense of buying something. He takes a book of photographs out of one of the tubs, gives it a cursory look, pays. He laughs, Tom has gone on filming while Wechsler returns the book and the seller gives him back his money. The seller is laughing as well, he says something I don't manage to catch. Wechsler wants to give him a tip, but the seller won't take it. Cut. Tom wanted to redo the scene because there was something the matter with the sound, but Wechsler adamantly refused. No, he said, I'll do it once but not twice. It may be possible to fake reality, but the fake can't be repeated. You'll just have to do the best you can with it. The mood was already a little soured. Wechsler approaches the camera, does something with his hand in his face, walks past the camera. Cut.

When the video is finished, it is set to automatically begin again, a loop, as though Richard were walking around and around in circles. The easy motion of his supple stride, which turns about the very smallest circle... Panther, panther, burning bright. I don't know how many times we watched the segment. Lots.

I'm put in mind of a piece of art by Bruce Nauman, a cassette recorder set in a concrete block. All that's left of it is the black wire disappearing into the concrete, but next to it is a sign that tells you the cassette is playing, that the recording on it is of a man screaming, a loop tape of an endless scream. You wonder if the tape hasn't worn out, the motor broken down, the loudspeaker blown, the man dead. To unplug the wire would be one solution. But is that what we're looking for—redemption? I have rarely seen a work of art that had such an effect on me. It was in Berlin.

Do you own a light-green raincoat?

How do you turn this thing off? asks Judith.

I move the mouse, the control panel appears, and I press stop.

I own a yellow rain jacket, says Judith.

When we were finished with the shoot and were waiting for Tom and Sascha, I went back to the bookseller and bought the catalog. As I was asking for it, the dealer seemed not to know what book I meant, or who I was. Then he pulled the fairly tattered copy from one of his crates, and demanded an insane price for it, which I paid without flinching. *The Family of Man.*

That's the catalog of a photo exhibition at the Museum of Modern Art, said Wechsler, who had surfaced alongside me. It must have been some time in the fifties, the show went on to tour halfway round the world. Pictures by a great many photographers, arranged by subject: birth, love, work, leisure, death, and so forth. After the war, there was probably a push to suggest the community of nations:

> *There is only one man in the world*
> *and his name is All Men.*
> *There is only one woman in the world*

and her name is All Women.
There is only one child in the world
And the child's name is All Children.

Perhaps a little on the grandiose side, but that's the fifties. At least they knew how to cut hair.

The last page of the book has been torn out. You can just see a corner of the picture with nothing discernible in the way of imagery, and the end of a quote and the name of the author:

…your footsteps…

Saint-John Perse

The final photograph in the exhibition was of an atomic explosion, said Wechsler, a warning to the peoples of the world. Was it also the last illustration in the catalog? Did the former owner tear it out for that reason?

A world to be born under your footsteps…

Hasten! Hasten! Word of the greatest Wind!

III

WE HAVE RETURNED

to our lives. We said goodbye at Zurich station, Judith had a tight connection, so there were no protracted farewells, just three kisses on the cheek, thank you for coming with me, it did me good. We'll keep in touch.

I watch her go, then she disappears among the other passengers, doesn't even turn around, and for an instant I feel very much alone. I've got nothing waiting for me beyond my houseplants, and they don't give me much affection. I drift through the station hall at half speed, get in the way, people barge me out of the way. Rush hour, indeed. A weary smile.

In the streetcar, I see a man who doesn't seem to have any better idea than I do of where to go and what to do. We look each other briefly in the eye, then look away, as though in shame.

It's cold in the apartment, before I left I turned the heating way down, now I turn it up. Just as well Tom and I have never lived together, so I could at least stay living where I was with no ill feeling, nothing needed sifting or sorting or removing or destroying. At that point I noticed that he left little trace in my life, not a postcard, no photo, no borrowed books, no dirty underwear to wash, no memories, not the least little thing. There was just his toothbrush to get rid of, and that wasn't before time either. I continue to be amazed by how long men hang on to their toothbrushes—or teethbrush? I wouldn't be completely surprised if Tom were to get in touch one day and ask for it back.

I go shopping, and take my time about it. It takes a while for the apartment to warm up. I think about maybe calling someone, but I don't really feel like talking. So it's buy some junk food for a solo evening in front of the tube.

My life goes around in circles, each day like the one before. Get up late, make coffee, a couple of hours of aimless busyness, lunch, more little bits of things in the afternoon that don't get anywhere, tidying, sorting, admin. If you've been on the planet for a while, it would be an easy thing to spend the rest of your life restoring order, filling in forms, filing bank statements, answering emails, reading saved newspaper articles. I make a cup of tea, browse through the supermarket rag, is there anything on offer that I could use? Detergent, coffee, salami, beer? Shopping. Shopping a second time because I forgot something, taking out the trash, watering the plants. I watch far too many serial killer videos. After I go to bed, I get up to check that I've remembered to lock the door.

THE LAST page of the catalog has unsettled me. Can it be that *The Family of Man* really ends with an atomic explosion and the apocalypse? I ordered the catalog from the public library, remarkably they had a copy, still more remarkably it was out on loan, and I had to wait ten days for it to be returned. Then the great relief: there's no mushroom cloud on the last page, just two little kids in rags. Hand in hand, they're walking down a forest path into a dazzling light. A world to be born under your footsteps.

I've ordered the poems of Saint-John Perse as well. I don't know the first thing about poetry, and the geezer did win the Nobel Prize for it, but if you ask me it's Grade A drivel. Someone getting intoxicated on the sound of his own rhetoric without any regard to meaning:

And it is time to build on the earth of men. And is a new germination on the earth of women.

Sounds a bit like watered-down Neruda, or that young woman who spoke at the inauguration of Joe Biden. Amanda Something.

I didn't take out either of the two books, I just put them straight back down the chute.

TWO WEEKS after Paris, I started in my new job. You have to enjoy those first moments, they don't come back: the first day at school, first love, first sex. This is your desk, here's your pen and pad of paper, here's a cup with a few sachets of chocolate and a couple of biscotti, a thermos flask with the company logo, and next to it a little card with Hey, Andrea! Welcome to our team! We're looking forward to working with you, and hope you have a fantastic start.

It's *Du* all around from one and all, young and old, boss and trainee, just like it is at IKEA. Here's your badge, your laptop, your password, get comfortable.

Later: This is the stationery cupboard. The abundance! Ballpoint pens in blue, red, and black, pencils, sharpeners, paper clips and bulldog clips in all sizes, Tipp-Ex, didn't know they still made that, glue sticks, scissors, staplers, all for the taking. I could open a store with pilfered office equipment.

Later: These are your new colleagues, she does this, he's responsible for that, and so on and on. And the tour of the office from the nice colleague: This is where we post outgoing mail, this is where the recycling goes, this is the small conference room, this is the large conference room. There are meeting points here, a copy machine and printer, and this is the kitchenette. Do you want a coffee? The machine works on your ID card. Here's where the boss's office is, shall we see if she's got a moment. Just to say hello.

At lunchtime in the canteen in the building next door, long tables, big windows facing out onto a green park with shaved lawns and majestic old trees. All the new people, the unfamiliar sounds and smells, it's quite exciting really, like a child's first day at school, but as early as tomorrow, it'll be habit.

There's the menu for the week ahead.

MONDAY

Meatloaf with gravy
Pasta and mixed root vegetables
or
Spinach-tofu loaf with mixed root vegetables

TUESDAY

Meatballs in curry sauce, served with
rice and mango chutney
or
Vegan meatballs in curry sauce, served with
rice and mango chutney

WEDNESDAY

Aberdeen Angus sausage with onion gravy
Buttered rösti and glazed carrots
or
Vegetarian sausage with onion gravy
Buttered rösti and glazed carrots

THURSDAY

Sautéed breast of turkey from the Alpstein,
accompanied with café de Paris sauce, buttered noodles,
and roast broccoli with nuts
or

Quorn schnitzel
accompanied with café de Paris sauce, buttered noodles,
and roast broccoli with nuts

FRIDAY

Pork schnitzel with pommes frites and
orange and purple carrots
or
Vegetarian schnitzel with pommes frites and
orange and purple carrots

Well, the cook's clearly no vegetarian. Plus a side salad and a small orange or apple juice, comes to nine fifty. Guests pay fourteen. But I'm not a guest. I'm a wholly owned subsidiary. Or what they call: being onboarded. I was pulled up on board, and now it's anchors aweigh. I hope our ship doesn't sink.

There ought to be a menu for the whole year, how calming that would be, to know on January 1 what you'll be eating in October or November.

A world to be born under your footsteps. Why can't I get that silly line out of my head?

OF COURSE the work is less interesting than making documentary films, but getting a check at the end of the month isn't to be despised either. And what a check! They're awash in money! I'm done with self-exploitation, from now on I'm just doing my forty-two hours a week, and if it's ever any more than that, I'll put in for overtime. If only it wasn't for all the damned meetings.

My nice new colleague explained the structure of the firm to me half a dozen times, but I still don't understand it, all the sectors and areas and teams with their snazzy names in English business-speak. Nor have I got used to viewing myself as a resource, human capital. My boss seems to be very happy with me. I'm no child of sorrow, and we have plenty of fun in our team, and I'm not afraid of hard work either. I don't tell anyone that it sometimes seems to me like a never-ending camp for grown-ups.

A kind of postlunch torpor seems to come over everyone here. They move in slow motion. If they move at all.

The view from the office is of the same park as the canteen, only we're a little higher up here, almost at treetop level. Golden autumn light floods in, the leaves have turned, they shift gently in the breeze, the first of them start to fall, and litter the gravel paths below. How nice it would be to be out there now, to warm up in the late-season sunshine, feel the wind, smell the decay. But we're a long way from all that up here, the windows are sealed. The air-conditioning is humming, set to the ideal temperature for the storing of office workers.

I go to the kitchenette. The clatter of the coffee machine, the whoosh of the dishwasher. The rinse cycle will end in one hour and twenty-three minutes. One hour and twenty-two minutes. One hour and twenty-one minutes. One hour and twenty minutes.

My nice new colleague joins me in the kitchenette, gets herself a coffee as well, helps herself to a cookie from the red cardboard packet, Lotus Biscoff caramel cookies, vegan, three hundred units, individually wrapped in clear plastic. I feel wrapped in clear plastic myself.

On her weekends, my nice new colleague goes hiking with her boyfriend. That's exactly what she looks like, too, a woman who would go hiking with her boyfriend. I wonder if they fuck? I'm sure they don't although they both would like to if they only dared. But I'm not going to cast the first stone, I don't have a boyfriend I go hiking with. Much less one I...

Where do you go hiking?

From Steg up the Hörnli and back, it's not a proper hike, more of a walk really.

What to say to that? That's all right. I haven't hiked anywhere in ages.

My nice new colleague helps herself to another cookie. Don't tell anyone, and winks at me.

Silence. One hour and seventeen minutes. One hour and sixteen minutes. Another twenty-three years. I must say, I thought life would be simpler.

The trick of it will be to convince myself of the importance of my work. But that's not going to be easy if what you do in office hours is read the newspaper. An interview with the German who served thirty-three years in a U.S. jail for a double murder, and was amnestied two years ago. He wrote a book about it. They all write books, why don't I write a book? Any life is worth telling. The man claims he is innocent. Aren't we all. And he says: I'm happy. And: My day-to-day life is perfectly normal now. I'm pleased for you! Perhaps I should spend thirty-three years in prison, to come to terms with my destiny? The trick of it will be to reconcile myself to my complete insignificance.

But I was insignificant before. Who cared about our films? Who watches things like that? What good do they do to the people who watch them? An author walks around in Paris, saying wise and stupid things. He stands at the tomb of Mr. and Mrs. Beckett and scratches his head; he pretends to buy the catalog from an exhibition. An author walks through the village he grew up in and reminisces about his childhood. He stands in the school where he learned to read and write, looking if anything more perplexed than the child that, aged seven, spelled out the nonsense that could be written in the handful of letters that he knew to decipher. John, meet Jane. He stands in the graveyard where his parents lie, and where, quite soon, he will come to be buried. It's cold and foggy, he's shivering. He hangs around the streets where he grew up. Passersby look at him suspiciously, they can all tell he doesn't belong there, that his intentions are dubious. He walks across the marketplace where in his youth they still sold cattle and that now is full of parked cars, and he sees an old woman with a walker who looks vaguely familiar to him. Now who was she again? More to the point, who was he?

Our desperate effort to find something in his past that might illuminate his subsequent life. Is the child father to the writer? He always liked to write, he got good marks in German, he was a bit of a loner. There are thousands just like that. He could have wound up in this office, could have spent his life processing sponsoring requests, sending out advertising leaflets, checking documents to see that they were as stipulated in the contract, with the company logo big enough and in the approved shade. Then sometimes he could have dreamed of the books he once wanted to write. Would the world have been poorer without them? Would his life have been poorer? Were his sacrifices worthwhile? The trick of it for him will have been to persuade himself that they were.

Wechsler walks through the streets where he grew up to the age of seven, with the camera dogging his heels. Our apartment was in the right-hand bottom corner, there where they've hung the washing out to dry. Four rooms off an interior corridor, a long balcony along the entire front, a view of what was then a meadow and is now built over. The playground still has the climbing frame, Wechsler remembers the taste of the metal when he licked it. Why in God's name would you lick a climbing frame? And the sandbox with the concrete surrounds, that's still there too, though the seesaw has gone.

He looks straight into the camera. What if we'd lived in the left-hand bottom corner, or the top right? Would that have changed anything? This whole autobiographical rigmarole, this so-called autofiction, what's it good for? That fake genuineness is the biggest lie of all. You never tell such whoppers as when you're talking about yourself. Anyway, we're still living, so do we have to get that in as well? Nothing has happened, nothing will last, and we've commemorated it. Why on earth? For me, literature was always the place where things happened, where I can have things take place that were never real and that I never did.

Yes, but we're not writing a book here, we're making a film.

True, Wechsler laughs, though it comes to the same thing.

Any life is worthy of being recorded. And anyway, you're the one who's always writing about ordinary people, people that no one notices.

But that's not reality, says Wechsler, freedom isn't in the material, it's in the way it's formed. The characters are interchangeable. You're interchangeable. We don't even know if you're blond or brunette or redhead, and if your eyes are blue or green.

How would you like me to be?

I'm certainly not going to tell you.

THE REQUESTS that came in today include: A world fistball championship. Fistball? Is that even a thing? A yodeling festival next summer, that's a big deal, we're certainly going to support that, a concert series of new music, fat chance, a couple of kids looking to get their first CD made, I don't think so. A promoter who has been putting on author events for ten years. Why do they say author readings, and not author/ess readings? Should I turn them down on the grounds of inadequate gendering? But the old programs they've enclosed are a fair balance, men and women in perfect harmony. Okay, you'll get a chance.

I am God. No one supervises me. I check the applications that are submitted, turn most of them down instantly, write standard rejections, take those that are possible with me into the meeting, and present them briefly. I always have one or two pet projects, but if the boss rejects those, I suck it up. I tried, what more can I do? That's sort of how I picture the Almighty: people pray to him and he gives them the thumbs-up or thumbs-down, depending on how he's feeling. He can't always say yes. And what criteria does he follow? Exemplary conduct is certainly not one.

I could get myself a dog. Or learn an instrument or a foreign language like Italian or Russian. I could write a book or try tango dancing. I could jump from a ten-meter board or become a missionary, but what would be my mission? I could buy a car and drive aimlessly around. I could sign up for a farm share, and pick up a crate of rightly unfashionable vegetables every week that I would drop in the organic dump at the end of the week, with the agreeable feeling I'd done something for the environment and the local farmers. I could feng shui my apartment. The next time I pick up my coffee, the washer's program is finished.

I'd better run out and buy something.

Did anyone hear me? Does anyone care? Will anyone check what time I clocked off? Will I ever clock on again?

I am sitting on a bench in the park. The bored mothers are standing by the playground. I could get myself pregnant. But who by? And what would that change? By the time the kid was born, it would be summer. And that would be too late.

A woman is sitting on a bench in the park. She's middle-aged, average height, medium build, moderately pretty, of unremarkable gifts. All around her are people with dogs, with children, businesspeople, old people, lots of people who know what they're about and where they belong, where they've come from and where they're going. The woman sits there, watching them, with an indifferent expression on her face. The camera reverse-zooms out, the woman gets smaller and smaller, and the park expands. If I were making the film, it wouldn't be allowed to end like that. So: to work!

WECHSLER COMES a day late. He has a good excuse. A flood in his basement, a railway strike, a sudden illness, no idea. At any rate, he's downstairs in the lobby now. I bump into him as I return from my walk with Judith, that first walk we undertook together.

And not before time.

Didn't you say the sound person was only arriving today?

So he doesn't have an excuse, he just got mixed up with the dates. Just as good.

Shall we have a drink together.

The bar is closed, says the night porter, who finally tracks down Wechsler's reservation and hands him the card for his room. You can order a drink from me, if you like.

It's not exactly cozy here, says Wechsler.

The young man's an expert on Baroque poetry, I hiss into his ear. No reaction.

I wouldn't mind getting my things upstairs, says Wechsler.

Why shouldn't I go upstairs with him? So far he's always behaved properly, and I'm sure he won't want to spoil things with me. I'm his biographer, after all. Or something of the kind.

His room is just the same as ours, only facing a different way. East, says Wechsler. He points to a one-family house that you can barely make out under a dim streetlight. One of the few structures in the Bauhaus style in Eastern Switzerland. Do I care? My GP's surgery used to be there. Must I know that? He used to prescribe the most delicious cough syrup. Aha. Do they still make that? Cough syrup? No idea. I'm not a great cougher. Cheers.

Are we going to fritter away our time on banal chitchat? But what's not banal?

Why do you write?

He laughs. Seriously? Lust, greed, and vanity.

Those are not your words, are they?

No, but they're pretty accurate.

We sit facing one another, me in an uncomfortable chair, him on the bed. He has taken off his shoes and is resting his legs on the bed. There are holes in his socks that he doesn't seem to be bothered about. One virtue of age is that you are no longer embarrassed about anything. At least that's how I imagine it. Wechsler pushes the pillows away and nestles back against the wall. Now we're even farther apart. I cross to the bed, scoot over would you, and sit down next to him. Our shoulders, hips, and knees are all touching. We both stare at the black rectangle of the

TV on the wall, as though that would provide the answer to all our questions. I pick up the remote on the bedside table, switch it on and mute the sound. A talk show, people getting heated, laughing, one is haranguing the others, you can tell from his superior expression and his needlessly emphatic gestures. Cut to the presenter, attempting to stop his flow. Wechsler takes the remote from me, clicks through a few stations, a sex scene, a car advert, the news, some people attempting to scale a fence. He switches it off.

It's like playing God, and I'm briefly not sure whether he's referring to writing or zapping. You can create new worlds, steer human destinies, make people fall in and out of love, cause children to be born, and people to die and be reborn, decide about their happiness and misery, life and death.

Why don't we have an affair?

That's your story, not mine, says Wechsler. You may imagine anything you like.

But what if it was your story, if I were your character, your creation, would there be something between us then?

No reply.

And what if I were Judith?

IT'S BEEN a while since I last googled David. And when I did it, it wasn't nostalgia or missing him or anything, I was just nosy about what had become of him.

David Schoch, still listed at the Department of Film Studies. That was where we first met, as students together, until I chucked it and took a job as a production assistant. I craved practice, he kept faith with theory. Now he's a lecturer, and I'm nothing. Art was always good at taking care of those who exploit it by teaching it or dealing with it on a theoretical level, not those who actually create it. But do I really want to teach the history of documentary filmmaking or nonrealistic forms of film narration? Apart from not knowing the first thing about them?

David's faculty page has his CV on it, so he's Dr. David now, and he has an imposing list of publications, divided among monographs, things he's edited, articles, essays, reviews, and lectures. I like to think the reason he's so successful is because I sent him packing. It's a possibility, isn't it, overcompensating? At any rate, it seems not to have killed him. The most recent publication of his is a thing called "Found Footage"—participatory documentary, as demonstrated on YouTube. I download the article, read the first half page of it, and then put it in the file for things I'm saving to read later, aka the trash. He has an email address.

I try to recall just how our relationship ended, was it reasonably harmonious or was there a big bang? But David wasn't a fighter, he was far too controlled, too intellectual, too mild, even. Presumably he had just been heartbroken while I was in bed with my new crush. I can't remember, though, I really can't. So here goes:

Hey David, it's been a while. Do you fancy going hiking with me next weekend? Cheers, Andrea.

I had to smirk when I pressed send. Pretty fresh, considering how I'd treated him. But then he was always a patient fellow—and you can imagine how that got on my nerves.

It seems he's up for a hike. Who'd have guessed. I got his answer a couple of hours later. Sure, why not, he doesn't have anything planned for the weekend. No reproaches, no sadness, he replies as though we're old buddies, nothing to it. That in turn bugs me somewhat, but then I started it, not him. A couple more emails back and forth, to deal with the practicalities. What about the Hörnli? Sure. And the timing, we'll meet in the second-to-last train car, and don't forget a rain poncho. He wrote that of the two of us he seems to be the more experienced hiker. What is a rain poncho? And what if my nice colleague and her boyfriend are on the same train? It would be a bit shaming, but they don't own the Hörnli, for God's sake.

SEX SCENES are boring, says Wechsler.

Says who?

It's like watching people eat. It just doesn't look very appetizing.

I try and think of some groovy sex scenes. It's not so easy. I once picked up *Fifty Shades*, well, I read quite a lot of it, to be frank. It was shockingly awful. Anastasia. His tongue lapped at my name...

Do you know the joke about the man from Appenzell who visits the brothel in Paris? Wechsler asks me, with the wrong expression for someone about to tell a joke. I groan, but not with pleasure. I can't abide jokes.

The man from Appenzell comes back from Paris, says Wechsler, and all his friends want to hear what it was like, and he tells them in lots of detail about the splendid establishment and the crystal chandeliers and the dark-wood paneling everywhere and the red velvet. He describes the beautiful women, the outrageous dresses they wear, their hairdos, their painted nails. He tells them how a woman approaches him and he buys her a glass of champagne— then he tells them how expensive the champagne is—he's Swiss, remember—and how the woman smiles at him, bats her eyes at him, charms him, and finally retires with him to a *séparée*. More description of more velvet and dark-wood paneling, dim lighting, a couch. Then he tells them how the woman gets undressed, how infinitely slowly, just the way he's telling it, in fact, her sophisticated underwear, stockings and garter belt, how she takes them all off, and how finally she's standing stark naked in front of him. The man's friends are all excited. And then? What happens then? Well, the rest, says the man from Appenzell, is pretty much like at home.

Wechsler doesn't laugh, and nor do I.

You are terrible at telling jokes, I say. At that he laughs. As do I.

And what if I were Judith?

They haven't seen each other for six months or a year. Judith doesn't ring the bell, she knocks on the door, even though she has a key. Richard opens it, she's standing there, beaming at him. He tries to speak, but she places a finger across her lips. Hush. They look at each other.

Judith is wearing tan-colored pants, a white sleeveless top, and sandals, around her ankle she has a fine gold chain she wears only for him. It wouldn't look good in the pulpit, she says once, and laughs. In fact, the chain is mine, but I lent it to her for the occasion.

Did you have a good trip?

She steps up to Richard, this time she places her finger across his lips, then puts her arms around him and kisses him. She breaks the embrace, precedes him into the living room, dropping her bag in the doorway, walks up to the wall of windows. Now he embraces her from behind, his hands on her hips, her belly. He kisses the back of her neck, her collarbone. He can't see her face, but he can tell she's smiling. He undoes her blouse, which has tiny, fiddly buttons, but they're in no hurry. He untucks her top, there's one more button, and then he takes it off her and lets it fall to the floor. She is wearing the pretty black undergarments he bought her the last time she visited. They went to the lingerie store together, nervous as a couple of teenagers buying condoms for the first time. When the young sales assistant asked them what they were looking for, Richard realized he didn't have the French terms. What can the salesgirl have thought? An elderly pair of lovers, were they sweet or were they embarrassing to her? Richard pushes a bra strap aside and kisses the spot where it marked her shoulder. Then he unclasps it and takes it off her, she raises her arms to help him. When he undoes her belt, she turns to face him, quickly unbuttons his shirt and pants, and brushes them off him. He stands naked in front of her, but not for long. Their tussling and holding and squeezing, their hunger for each other. Judith takes her hands off him for a moment, walks to her bag, pulls out a bottle of water and takes a drink. Richard has a chance to look at her. Sometimes she makes remarks on things she doesn't like about herself physically, and he can see what she might mean, but looking at her now, he's blind to all of them, and she's nothing more nor less than the woman he loves. And the rest is just like at home.

I've lain down and am lying next to Wechsler, who's still sitting up against the wall, sipping at his beer and staring at the black screen.

Why don't we have an affair? True, he's a good bit older than me, not my typical victim profile, but the age difference isn't that much, and I don't have to marry him. Physically, he seems reasonably okay, now that he's no longer dead, but that's not the attraction. So what is? Maybe the fact that he doesn't seem needy, doesn't go trotting after me like a dog with his tongue hanging out. Maybe it's the fact that he has a story and a secret that are big enough not to be given away at a first meeting. Is it called necrophilia if you imagine sex with a dead person? But in my imagination he's still alive.

Finally, he lies down beside me, we lie facing each other, very close, looking into the other's eyes, for a long and thrilling moment. He lays his hand on my hip, kisses me quickly on the mouth, just a touch. What am I wearing for this? Not jeans, you can't take them off with any dignity. A dress he can push up, maybe? Too easy, too quick.

Maybe a belted skirt, not too short, a blouse, stockings. Black underthings.

And do you still find sex scenes uninteresting?

Not in reality or in imagination, says Wechsler, only in literature.

Shall we use *Du*, I ask.

No, he says, and starts to unbutton my blouse.

DAVID IS looking good, much better than he used to. I mean, of course he looks the same, but he's gotten to be more confident, which makes a huge difference. He appears comfortable with himself, looks out into the world, only those weird pants with pockets up and down the legs are a bit of a turnoff. But I'll ignore those for now, after all we're going hiking, and plus fours would have been worse. On the other hand, he seems to have lost the shy, questioning, dreamy aspect of himself. He's no longer the uncertain, unhappy young man who was in love with me, but a successful and confident academic, off the shelf.

He gets up, kisses me on the cheek, smiles. Good to see you.

You can forget about the first hour when we were on the train, we're just filling each other in about what's happened, what we've been doing, how things stand, nothing important. I cut to the chase: Doesn't your girlfriend object to you hiking with your ex? He: I don't have a girlfriend just now. Oh. What about your boyfriend? he grins. Okay, I suppose I could have asked if you have one. And have you stopped making films?

The failure of the Richard Wechsler documentary was the last straw. Even before that, things weren't going too well. Who can live off filmmaking in Switzerland?

In Steg I spot my nice colleague and her boyfriend walking by on the platform, they must have come on the same train as us, and they're completely dressed for the mountains, in functional clothing, I think they call it, with rucksack, big boots, and those Nordic walking sticks. The man looks like a bit of a dullard, but I can't really explain why. Is it his facial expression? His movements? The color of his garments? Or just the fact that he's hiking with a slightly dull woman? I pretend to have to relace my boots to let them get a start on us. But I needn't have been so fastidious: the way they steamed off, we have no chance of ever catching up to them.

Four hundred thirty-nine meters of altitude can feel like a lot. Easy hike, no special difficulties, the Internet said. I ought to sue whoever posted that for bodily harm. David is continually kept waiting for me. Can't he adjust to my pace? Or is he embarrassed to be passed by oldsters? If you just stop by the side of the path you can pretend to be admiring the view. Of course oldsters are fitter than me, they can spend all their time hiking. There's no chance of conversation during the ascent, the most I manage is panting for water sometimes, because David has agreed to carry my rucksack.

There's a restaurant a little way below the summit, but we've brought our own food with us, in the style of proper hikers. There's a wide meadow between the restaurant and the summit where people are dotted about, picnicking. We see a place we like when I hear someone calling me. My nice friend from work has spotted me. So I go up to her and say hello. You gave me the idea, but hey, the mountain's big enough for all of us. This is David. Pleased to meet you. This is Rüdiger. Ah, from Germany. Nice. Why do I say that? Why is it nice if she goes hiking with a German guy? Do you want to join us? Sure, says David, always polite. No, I say, we have something we need to talk about. I'll see you tomorrow in the office. I'm sure they don't screw.

We find a spot on the edge of the meadow, close to the vast electronic mast with a thousand antenna dishes on it.

So what do we need to talk about? asks David.

If we'd brought sausages, we could have fried them in the electric smog.

Seriously, now, says David, you get in touch after I don't know how many years, and you want to go hiking? What do you really want?

I've no idea. That's the truth, I've no idea. That woman down there with her German fellow, I point vaguely in the direction of my nice friend from work, fifty yards below us, she gave me the idea of going hiking with a friend. It seems that that's what single women my age like to do.

David laughs and shakes his head. Ha, well, I always knew you were a bit crazy.

Do you suppose those two are fucking? Or are they just hiking partners?

David looks at me severely. Andrea, please! Then he looks back at my nice friend from work again, and at her Rüdiger. I think you're probably right.

But we fuck. Not there of course, later on, at David's. Tasteful apartment. Instead of books, hundreds of DVDs, arranged alphabetically by director. Is that relevant? I guess so, because we went on to talk about filmmaking. But only later. We lie crosswise on his bed, his head resting on my stomach, my hand doing something around his upper thigh.

Say, your writing, all those articles, is anyone interested?

He can't concentrate properly. No idea. Maybe other people in film studies?

But does it have any effect on new films being made? Would it have something to teach me? Inspire me, maybe? I mean, if I were to read any of it.

He has just now got something else on his mind, for which I may be responsible.

I thought you weren't making films anymore.

I'm a filmmaker who doesn't make films. In the age of YouTube.

He moans. So you did read my article.

The first bit of it.

It would probably have been easier to make a film on a dead author.

He's dead now, isn't he.

I pull myself up and sit astride David. He closes his eyes.

And then you write something nice about it.

Too much dialogue. Fast-forward.

AFTERWARD. WE did talk about films. We're lying naked, side by side, David is absentmindedly stroking my bottom, which irks me, and I roll onto my back. He is telling me about documentary film production with mass participation, which happens to be his current research topic. He's really in his element now, the professor, apart from the fact that he's lecturing in bed naked. Secretly, I think I understand much more about filmmaking than he does; after all, I've made a couple that didn't turn out too badly. One of them even won an award. But David has read Bakhtin and Eco and all those Frenchies I can't tell apart. I can't put up much of an argument.

One French artist gave thousands of interviews all over the world, Professor David is just telling me, where people asked him the same questions each time, what is love, what is the meaning of life, what is happiness? And he made a film out of his answers.

And were there any good ones?

That isn't the point, says David. ARTE television put out a series of *Twenty-Four Hours* films on various cities. Then YouTube suggested its users film themselves on a particular day, and from the clips they were sent they put together a ninety-minute film called *Life in a Day*. They've now done it twice, ten years apart.

But don't people do that anyway? YouTube is nothing but a gigantic agglomeration of uploads on everything from kittens to serial killers. The algorithm does duty as the editor.

Every minute, five hundred hours of video are uploaded onto YouTube, says David, and those are old numbers. If you were to spend your entire life in front of your computer, twenty-four hours a day, then you could just about get across a single day's output.

He's taken his laptop off the bedside table and turned to YouTube. I roll onto my front. I think he's a bit embarrassed about his preferences, workout videos and *Fast & Furious* trailers. What's with that?

But he's opened *Life in a Day*, and we're into July 25, 2020, with a dog barking, a couple of children being born, and a man and a woman driving to Kansas City in a blue car. A man who jumps into a lake in the north of Siberia, saying his big fear is his life going by unnoticed by others, which is probably a well-founded fear in the north of Siberia. There are some proposals on that day and some weddings, a fair number of kisses, small dogs, big elephants. Like *The Family of Man*, only less well shot. A film as boring as life. What are we doing watching it? These strangers, in no way more interesting or nicer to look at than we are. But perhaps we see ourselves in them, they are stand-ins for us, and as they become important and deathless, so do we.

Didn't anyone fuck on that day?

There are other sites for that kind of thing, says David. Would you prefer that?

I would not.

These conceptual things are of course much more interesting to theorists than any well-made conventional documentary, even if they're basically rubbish. They can reflect on them and set up theories and witter on about the future of documentaries and the crisis of the documentary.

Documentary isn't what matters in these projects. It's like Carnival, it's not the result, it's participation. Carnival has its own rules, it's a time of fun and renewal for everyone to join in.

For those who like that sort of thing, I say. I hate Carnival.

David is looking for a particular point in the film that he seems to know by heart.

There's an Asian-looking woman cooking; her friend behind the camera is asking her what she's cooking. Fried eggplants and peppers, she says. And that she wants to leave him, because he takes their relationship for granted, and is never going to marry her. He doesn't react, just goes on filming. Now the woman laughs disbelievingly, hang on, are you okay with that? I thought you were just saying it for the film, says the man softly, as though not wanting it to be on the soundtrack. No, I'm serious. The woman's laughter changes to tears. Oh, that is sad, says the man miserably, while continuing to film. The woman has turned away, she is wiping her eyes with the back of her hand. The man continues to film.

David looks at me and grins. And I'm thinking he's every bit as much of an asshole as the guy filming his weeping girlfriend, even if he's never to my knowledge held a camera in his hand.

Wechsler and I often used to talk about the meaning and meaninglessness of filming. He told me how the electronics shop in his village used to have a camera in the window whose signal was transferred straight onto a monitor, and when they were kids, they all used to stand and stare at themselves in the monitor. The worst mirror would have given a better image, but that wasn't what it was about. The monitor was a further dimension, said Wechsler, a fiction that lifted us out of our everyday lives.

David says something rather similar: basically, all these projects were about time passing. One of the ARTE people put it this way: Nothing will remain, and that's what we wanted to capture.

Then what about the films I made? Will anything remain of them? Will anyone be interested in Wechsler a hundred years from now? I kind of doubt it. And what about our film, if we had managed to make it?

When I first met David, I was just making my first film, the portrait of one of the cleaning ladies at the university, Emina, a Bosnian, I had managed to make friends with. That was because, while I was still a student, I used to sit in the library until late, so I got to know all the cleaning staff. The film turned out quite well, even though there was an element of social romanticism about it, a bit of poor-but-happy kitsch. Also: every human being deserves our interest, any life is worthy of being recorded. As though that were a kindness. I even got a subsidy for it, which I kept. Emina and her husband came to the award ceremony, and enjoyed the attention, but I never shook the feeling I'd taken advantage of them. After that, I made mostly documentaries about artistic types, because they were all self-promoters and narcissists anyway.

I think David was always a bit envious of my filmmaking. First he showed it by showering me with praise and calling me a genius, then by picking over every detail of my films, every single shot, but never as honest criticism, only as a proposal, a note, an idea, a suggestion of how it might have been done differently. Just say if you think my work is shit. Make one of your own. Perhaps that was why I left him, too, and not the possessive esoteric I left him for.

ANDREA AND David, an account of a failed relationship. It wasn't sex, anyway, we were always compatible there. But eventually you have to get out of bed. If I were making such a film, I would shoot us both walking, David always a step and a half ahead, lecturing. Go from right to left. And of course David would go from right to left, while I would go from left to right. And he was possessive as well. The times he wasn't walking in front of me, he was always holding my hand. I didn't want to hold hands. I don't even like the idea: I wanna hold your hand. It sounds like something you'd say to a dog, shake hands, and I wasn't his dog. When we watched a film together, I could guess what scenes he'd bring up later, could even hear the words he'd use: This is a reference, Godard, remember, it was in *Le Mépris*. Why couldn't he use the English version of the title? *Contempt.* I knew he was brainier than me, and that he had French. Also English, a bit of Spanish, and maybe Italian and Swedish and Finnish as well. But was that the truth? What would the film have been like, if he'd made it, about me, the woman he loved? Whom he would certainly say he loved?

Me in front of the window against the light, I'm wearing something shimmery and translucent, the light picks out the contours of my form. Dreamy piano music, David's voice-over, soft, as though talking to himself. His tongue laps at my name.

David thought I was highly talented. Sure, we didn't do it for less. Also children only existed in two versions, highly talented or disturbed, but either way they have to be something out of the ordinary. Highly talented, basically, only means she hasn't accomplished anything. I think I'd rather have been disturbed or maybe mildly sociopathic. At any rate, I was as sure then as now that I wasn't or am not highly talented, nor will I ever be.

The next morning, I know I have made a mistake. David has got up early, bought croissants and fresh orange juice and flowers. No roses, thank God, just asters, for the season. When I step out of the shower, he's sitting at the table grinning like a loon. Whatever a loon is. I sit down naked at the breakfast table, and he gives me a look. Presumably it's unsanitary or inappropriate or something.

In many ways, he reminds me of Tom, except that Tom, to be frank, was a loser. He satisfies me in bed, he's intelligent, deferential, has good taste, a well-paid job. And he's in love with me. All those wanting me to go back to him, raise your hands! Is that all? Well, sayonara.

I once had an affair with a man with a beard. I didn't like the beard and told him so. The next time we met, he had shaved it off. I chucked him. I once had an affair with another man with a beard. I didn't like the beard, and told him so. The next time we met, he still had it. That didn't last much longer either. Men, a lesson for you! An excerpt from Andrea's wit and wisdom: If you have a beard your girlfriend doesn't like, then either shave it off or keep it on, neither will avail you.

I need to go now. Yes, sure, I'll call you. It was nice. Are the flowers for me? Thanks. All the best.

I drop the flowers in the nearest bin. What if David should see them? Who cares, then at least my WhatsApp will come as less of a shock to him. Perhaps I don't love him enough. Or at all.

EVERY DAY now, I cycle into work, even though the weather's turned cold already. That's the high point of my day. I bought a cap and gloves and some special rain gear, a kind of tent that goes over my handlebars, dark blue with luminous stripes. I wanted one in pale green, but they didn't have that. It's early when I set out, only just getting light. It's been raining, and the damp roadway reflects the lights, the noise, the rain splashes up in my face. So much freshness. There are sodden leaves lying there, one corner I skidded and almost went over.

Problems at work. It's not work that's the problem, it's me. The way I swank around with my films in front of the others annoys me. Me, the artist, I'm better than you. They tolerate me, but I'm not tolerable. I'm often in a mood, really snarky. I asked my nice friend how Rüdiger's getting on. The name, even! If I had to come up with a German, I'd call him Rüdiger. Or Holger. He's fine, she says. And then I asked her if he's fucking her, not in so many words, but she got my drift all right. I really shouldn't have done that. She started to cry, and then I had to listen to the whole sad story, which doesn't change anything, so let's leave it out. At any rate, I seem to have become her confidante, and she wants to have lunch with me in the canteen, although I'd much rather grab a soggy schnitzel sandwich or a pizza baguette at the mart to eat at my desk. Without bothering to clock off, of course. The boss noticed and called me in. She was very respectful and diplomatic, didn't want it to sound like a rebuke. She appreciated that after being self-employed for so long, I wasn't familiar with office timekeeping. But she would be glad all the same if...the nice smile.

Half the time, I don't know what to do with myself. All the others seem to have some tricks or knack of keeping themselves busy, at any rate they're sitting at their desktops, typing rapidly, with intense expressions. For a while, I try YouTube videos, but interviews with serial killers are no fun with the sound off. So I go down the Google rabbit hole.

Thrilling detail from the life of the three-toed sloth: they live symbiotically with a species of moth that likes to nest in their fur and lay eggs in their excrement. The moths supply the sloths with nitrates and phosphates, which stimulate the growth of algae. The sloths eat the algae during grooming, thus giving them important nutrients not contained in the rest of their sparse diet of leaves. And once a week, they climb down from their trees to poop.

How much time can an employee credibly spend in the little girls' room? My colleagues must think I have irritable bowel syndrome. The Internet says employers don't need to pay for bathroom visits. I hope my boss doesn't cotton on to that.

The weather in Paris, cloudy, four degrees. The weather in Moscow, arctic flurries, one degree, the weather at the South Pole, sunny and dry, minus thirty-nine. I wish I could be at the South Pole, filming penguins.

I'm bothered by all the requests for sponsorship that come in every day, more and more of them, mostly from artistic types. The things they come up with. And we're supposed to foot the bill. Even though it says unambiguously in the guidelines: artistic projects by individuals are not eligible for support. Can they not read? I've got the reputation of being especially severe on film projects. That may be, but there's just so much crap. And if a thousand people see it in an art house cinema, that's not exactly having a major cultural impact. Once or twice, former colleagues got in touch with me directly and begged, no dignity. But I always turned them down flat. I said we followed a one-brand strategy and their project violated the brand. Whatever that means. Perhaps I can send you a couple of publicity pens or a banner or two.

In a word: Could be better.

FOG. SOMETIMES I take myself to places, just so I don't have
to sit around at home. An exhibition in a provincial town,
an artist I have time for. Apart from me, there isn't a soul
there. It gets dark surprisingly early. Fog in the streets of
the little town, even though it's a Saturday, no one around.
I take the train back through the dark landscape, the occasional lights, a station with a name I can't read, a street
running parallel to the tracks, only slowly and then very
suddenly to go off on its own, an empty soccer field under
floodlights, a brightly illuminated industrial scene.

Back in my apartment it's cold. I sit on the side of the
bed, chug red wine from the bottle, a bit theatrically, I'll
admit, watch videos on my smartphone. I'm bored, alone.
I'd like to have someone like Richard or Judith back in my
life. Sure, they annoyed me from time to time, but whenever I was with them, I had the feeling that what I was
doing with my life had some relevance. Just like the events
in a good book, which make sense and are more than just a
chapter of accidents, the way my life was. I lie down, close
my eyes, and whisper: Come back, come back! It's like a
séance, an invocation of spirits.

There they are, I'm in a vast, brilliantly lit hall in a cas-
tle. I'm wearing a hooped skirt and heels. Music fills the
space, it sounds like a storm, and Richard and Judith come
waltzing in. The other couples melt away, clear a path for
them as they come dancing directly toward me. Then suddenly the three of us are dancing, I don't even know how

that's possible, but it happens apparently effortlessly. We float through the air, laughing, beneath us everyone else is dancing again, and seems to have forgotten us. We are ecstatic, ecstasy binds us, ecstasy sustains us, we are one.

When I wake up, I don't know what time it is. I'm in my day clothes, which are all rumpled. I need a pee, and have a cow's thirst. As I get up, I knock over the empty wine bottle on the floor.

Outside, there's still dense fog. I have trouble remembering what happened yesterday, and then the past few days and weeks and months; I feel as though I've woken up in a void, as though my whole previous life had been a dream now melting away in the murk of day.

The kitchen doesn't seem familiar to me either, it takes me ages to find the coffee, the filter papers, the coffeepot. After, I head outside. There's no one at all around. I've left my phone behind, I don't know if it's morning or afternoon. I'm in some part of town I've never been before, I walk along a wide road flanked by factories, offices, a clump of apartment blocks. I sit down on a bench at a bus stop, the green wooden slats are covered with water droplets from the fog. I have a wet bum, and it's cold. I walk on. Is it getting dark already, or is there something the matter with my eyesight?

I turn back, always on the same road, till I see where I am. In the lobby of my building, there's a notice from the management. The subject line is Fresh Air. Tenants are requested not to leave windows open for too long to save on heating costs. There's a PS where the management wishes everyone Compliments of the Season and a Merry Christmas. Is it that late already?

My mailbox contains a begging letter from an orphanage and a flyer. On the front page, the headline: Remember to put your clocks back. Summertime is over.

I PUT all the clocks back, my wristwatch, my alarm, the clock on the landline phone, the one on the stove. I feel better now. It's noon, I should eat something, but I'm not at all hungry.

My phone rings. It's Judith. She's left her husband, well now, there's a thing, and she asks if she can maybe come and stay with me for a few days.

I picture it. Judith is back from church, not as a minister this time, but as a congregant, if that's a word. A member of the audience, anyway. Afterward, she looked in on the cemetery briefly, even though it's not All Souls until tomorrow. Richard's grave is still new, the stone has not been put in yet, there might be a withered-looking wreath, but it's not likely, as the cemetery custodians have tidied everything up for November, the month of the dead, and planted the graves freshly for winter, with heather and mums.

Judith doesn't say much at lunch. There's soup and bread, as always on Sundays when there's not much time for cooking. Then the girls disappeared into their rooms, and Judith's husband pours two cups of coffee from the French press and brings one to Judith. She stands in front of the window, a dark silhouette against the fall garden. If this were a film, I would cut here, the conversation is so painful, no one needs to hear it. No one should either, it's a private matter.

Judith's husband doesn't understand, presumably Judith doesn't either. The thing with Richard could have been talked out and processed between them, maybe her husband had something with a fellow teacher or the mother of a pupil. It would have left a scar, but where's the relationship that has no scars? Judith's husband tried to talk to her, change her mind, then he gives up and goes out in the garden. He rakes the leaves, he has to do something. A nice scene: the bare garden in the fog, the sopping lawn, the yellow and brown leaves, the rotting and shriveling, the miserable man with the long rake. Piano music, maybe Satie, something meditative and quiet. Whoever is alone now will long remain so.

Did Judith tell the children? Surely. She went up to their floor. What's been going on here? she says as she sets foot in Ann's room, can you at least make the bed? She calls Ella. Will you come here a moment.

The girls don't understand either, but they don't ask for reasons. Perhaps they can sense that there's another man, and they don't want to know. What would they think if they knew he's existed for a long time, and is now dead? That he could be their father? Ella cries, Ann hugs her. They look like a couple of drowned rats. What's going to happen? I'm just going to go away for a few days. I need to get away, have some time to myself. Don't worry, I'll be back, okay?

But where will she go? A hotel? A room in the parish sick bay? This is when she calls me from her bedroom, even though she no longer has any secrets, and doesn't need to hide. But the whole mechanics of separation are painful. Why me, doesn't she have any friends in the village, any confidantes who will stand by her and take her in? But she's the minister there, and it would be a minor scandal. It is a minor scandal. Or not so minor.

Sure, just come, I'll be here.

I don't ask any questions. She'll send me a WhatsApp message when she knows what time her train gets in. Maybe I'll collect her at the station.

I picture her packing an overnight case, just the bare minimum. She puts in her pretty underwear, maybe she's worried her husband will find it? Or else because it's virtually the only thing she has that reminds her of Richard? She packs the book of Jewish mysticism as well.

Judith is scatterbrained, she forgets her toothpaste, almost forgets her reading glasses. She says goodbye to her girls, that's perhaps the hardest thing of all. They're still huddled in the room together, they seem to have spoken, they look at her with timid expressions, as though hoping she might have changed her mind. Judith hugs them silently, first one then the other, there's something almost official about it, like a state visit or the opening of a new airport. She gives them some last-minute instructions, mentions the leftovers in the fridge they need to heat up for supper. Look after Dad. As she goes down the stairs, her legs feel like they're made of lead.

She goes out into the garden, talks briefly to her husband. We see them both through the window of the living room, can't hear what they're saying, their expressions are grave, they look tired, once Judith smiles briefly, and then so does her husband. Cut.

On the train, she doesn't know how she ought to be feeling. She's sad but also relieved, incredibly relieved, happy, unsure, confused. Just after Frauenfeld, the sun breaks through the clouds. I'm already on my way to the station. A bathing beauty smiles at me from a poster in the window of a travel agency: All the sun you could ever wish for. Daft slogan.

THE LAST time by the sea. Wechsler had asked me to Trouville. He's already there. Why had he taken the earlier train? He collects me from the station, he's already marked by his illness, but he still insists on walking to the hotel. We walk along the pier. The river has almost no water, it's ebb tide, and the fishing boats are lying on their sides in the mud.

It's a small hotel on the front, he must have been here with Judith, but he doesn't say so, too much the gentleman. Of course we share a room. Twin beds or a double? asks the receptionist. Double, says Wechsler quickly, he doesn't even ask me. I would have said the same. We have no time to lose.

Even though we've only been walking for fifteen minutes, Wechsler is exhausted. He wants to have a lie-down, then he can show me the town. He lies on the bed in shorts and socks. I get undressed and lie beside him. It's nice with him, slow, calm, but intense. It turns me on for some reason that he still uses the formal *Sie*, it gives our time a curious dignity and seriousness. He doesn't take his eyes off me, and I see the blue in them, the mercurial, elusive blue. He looks very concentrated, almost earnest, as though this thing we're doing is the hardest and most important thing in the world.

Again, I have the feeling he's emptying me, but this time it doesn't bother me. I would give him some of my vivaciousness if I could. Perhaps I can, perhaps that's exactly what I'm doing. And what about him? He takes something away from me, gives me something back. Just what it is and what use I have for it is my own business.

The last time by the sea. We walk along the promenade, a plank boardwalk that first runs parallel to the coastal road and then, when that turns off into the interior, over the sand between the sea and the first line of buildings. The houses and hotels are on a bluff, slightly elevated. In some places, the sand has completely covered the boardwalk. There aren't many people about, the season is over or hasn't yet begun. We sit on a bench, gaze out to sea, don't speak.

Is home the place you come from, or where you want to go to? Wechsler says finally. It's one of those questions that don't require an answer, or to which no good answer exists. Silence brings us closer than speech.

In the evening we eat shellfish on the terrace of a bistro. It's my first time eating oysters, and presumably

Wechsler's last. I look at him and parrot his movements. He seems happy.

Every time I eat oysters in the future I'll think of you, I say, and this evening with you. And then I feel annoyed with myself. He's not dead yet.

The next day is mild for the season, and we eat breakfast outside. Wechsler surprises me with his appetite. He asks me if I'd like to go swimming. He slept badly, and I woke up a couple of times from his restlessness. The T-shirt he slept in was soaked with sweat. He woke up very early and sat by the window. I pretended I was still asleep, then I did fall asleep, and woke up late. We almost missed breakfast.

Ebb tide. We have to walk a long way to reach the water. It's icy cold, and the fact that it deepens so gradually doesn't make it any easier. Wechsler takes my hand, and we walk on in together until we're in up to our hips. Then we launch ourselves into it. The cold makes us gasp.

We lie on our towels. A few clouds have appeared, and there's a mild breeze. I'm cold, and press myself as flat as I can to the ground. I stay cold all day, even though I pull on a heavy sweater later.

I stand in the window, naked but for said pullover. Wechsler comes up behind me and puts his arms around me. We stay standing there like that, gazing at the sea, which is now very close.

I leave a day early. Wechsler would have liked me to stay, but I can't.

Are you sorry you've come?

Not for a single second. But it's time to go now.

That's how it might have been. The last time by the sea.

ON MY way to the station, I'm briefly irritated with myself. What am I doing with Judith and Richard? Why don't they leave me in peace, both in my head and my life? I remember the first video we shot with Wechsler in the museum. When he was talking about Vallotton: The artist is like a lover, touching the model or the landscape and touched by them. The painting is an act of love, a celebration of beauty.

Have I touched Richard? Has he touched me? Which of us is the artist, and which the model? Could it be that it's not him that's the point, or Vallotton, but me? Was it all about me from the very beginning? Then, why? Why me? And is it a pleasing thought, or disquieting, even frightening? I am Richard's inheritance, a character he didn't finish writing, left to wander in the limbo of unrealized novel figures, not knowing what to do with herself.

I take my phone out and film myself in the tram, staring at my peculiar features on the wretched little screen. Behind me, I see a man make a face and go and sit somewhere else.

Judith hasn't come with a bag but a little wheeled suitcase, with which she settles in. I've made some space for her in the closet, and show her the bathroom, the kitchen, where to find tea and coffee, she doesn't take sugar and I don't have milk. She will sleep on the sofa, one of those put-you-up things that allows you to convert an uncomfortable sofa into an uncomfortable bed. In terms of physical comforts, I'm sure she wishes she were back home. Now she can see how the creative precariat lives. Well, let's not get too sorry for ourselves, I could afford a bigger apartment, not least now I have my swank job. But I like this monkish life. Can a life be nunnish, or just monkish?

And now? We go for a walk.

Very near where I live is a huge cemetery, but because people these days prefer to be cremated, it's turned into more of a park with old trees, nature meadows, benches. There are lots of cemeteries in his books, so we're in a familiar place, Wechsler Country.

It's cold, for the first time this fall, there's a sense of winter in the air. But the sun's shining; the autumn colors, the smells, the chill on your skin, it's a delight. No, delight is for springtime. It's magnificent. The cemetery gardeners are blowing the leaves, there are two huge piles of them already near the entrance. Maybe it would be a job for me.

Just like at the office, they have various departments here as well, and the graves are numbered. Not even the dead can escape this country's mania for organization. Someone has put a slug barrier around one of the graves.

We walk along a gravel path between huge arborvitae hedges that feel as though they're crushing us. Judith is quiet and has a serious expression. I ought to feel sorry for her, I can see how she's suffering, but I can't share her suffering. As far as I'm concerned, it's a Sunday afternoon like any other, even a little bit nicer than most, because I have company and I like Judith. I film her on my phone, smiling faintly under the arborvitae, looking a little resigned. Is she already regretting leaving her husband and family?

The crematorium has something of a heathen temple look, I can't quite say why. There is something lifeless and outsize about it, I'm sure it's colder in there than it is outside, but the doors are locked. There is an inscription on the lintel that we have some trouble reading: Flame, destroy the ephemeral, free the eternal. It doesn't sound quite Christian to me. What religion has the cult of the eternal flame? Is it Zoroastrianism? Not even Judith knows. Google it. No, don't google it.

By the entrance some black-clad persons have assembled, the men are smoking, a few children are running around shouting, until a young woman tells them in a foreign language to stop. Someone must have died, we're not wanted here, this isn't our tragedy.

We pass on through the rows of graves, study the gravestones, read the names of the deceased. Here is a married couple, both dead in the same year, there are father and son presumably sharing one grave. Where is the mother? The ornamentation of the graves is no more tasteful than that of most apartments, a lot of convention, a lot of kitsch. There is heather on almost all of them. Heather is hardy and inexpensive.

Near the exit, we find the graves of Gottfried Keller, don't know, haven't read much of him, and Johanna Spyri, I only know the old film version, with, what was he called

again, the old potato-nosed actor? In black and white.
More heather.

I feel a bit like Heidi in the city, says Judith, both sad
and excited. She takes my arm.

Does that make me Herr Sesemann, then? Or Fräulein
Rottenmeier?

Thanks for letting me stay, says Judith.

She doesn't want to talk about the family, she'd rather
talk about Richard. How long did the relationship go on
for? She doesn't like the word relationship. Love affair,
correct, that's what she called it when we were up the
mountain. Or just love. How long did their love last? Almost twenty years. Longer for him.

IT BEGAN in a cemetery, we were both at a classmate's funeral. I don't know why we went, neither of us was especially close to him. But Richard was visiting his parents,
and I felt like seeing old friends again. I had just got a new
job near Lake Constance, and didn't really know anyone
there. Maybe I just wanted to see him again.

And that trip to Paris with the butcher and the other
man? When you and Richard shared a room?

She looks at me, her face betrays nothing. Who told
you about that?

It happens in one of Richard's books.

That was nothing, says Judith curtly.

Am I supposed to believe her? Why would she lie to
me? Perhaps she took one of the other men back to her

room and...? Perhaps it was the butcher, and Richard caught them at it? She does seem a bit flustered anyway. She gathers herself, tries again.

All right, it was my classmate's funeral. To be honest, I had a little crush on him once. Then he started doing drugs. He went to India, came back, couldn't adjust. And then he died from a rare illness, there were all kinds of rumors and reports. But that's not what's at issue here.

There weren't many people present that I knew. Richard and I found each other right away, we sat together during the service. There was something in the air. Afterward, there was a little reception, with lots of wine and nothing really to eat. Richard and I stood in a corner talking about old times, and then he said did I want to walk? I've got to get out.

We were both a bit tipsy, I think. We headed down to the river, it was springtime. Richard was already fairly successful, and I'd be lying if I said that hadn't impressed me. And he was a listener. I think I talked practically the whole time, and he said very little.

We walked past the old school building, then along the canal, there's a little stable where I used to ride out when I was a girl. We stopped to look at the horses, who were very friendly and came up to us by the fence. Richard stroked one on the head and withers and I had the feeling he was stroking me on the head and neck!

Then there was a piece of woodland going along by the river. It's the middle of the day, quite deserted. We go into the woods, the leaves are not yet fully out, the ground is dappled with sunlight. The path leads straight through the woods, but Richard leaves it for no reason I can see, makes his way through the undergrowth, which then starts thinning out. I'm coming after him. At this stage, I think neither of us knows why we've left the path, and are tripping over the uneven ground. Eventually, Richard comes to a stop, it's not really a clearing, just somewhere the trees are a little less densely packed, and the sun is very bright, shining down on us like a beam. Richard turns back and looks at me silently. I go toward him, I mean to stop, but I go right up to him, in the end he practically can't help but put his arms around me and hold me. We made love there in the forest. I tried not to think about anything.

On the way back on the train, I got completely undressed in the toilet, and wiped away all the little bits of twig and leaf that were sticking to me. Someone knocked on the door several times, and when I was finally done and came out, an old man was standing there and was very angry with me. I just thought it was incredibly funny. Strange that I can remember him so well, but not how Richard and I made love there in the woods.

And not long after, your older daughter was born.

Judith doesn't say anything. Is Richard the father of Judith's daughter, then? Did she tell him? Why am I bothered either way? Do I feel like I'm the milkman's daughter? Is Richard my father or something? All milkman's children have the same father, after all.

The following years we would write occasionally, but not often, says Judith. Richard told me he loved me, and I rebuffed him more or less gently, explained why I couldn't go on writing to him, and yet still kept on writing to him. He sent me copies of his books with suggestive inscriptions that I cut out and kept hidden in a drawer. And then we saw each other at a reading he was giving locally, and I went, and afterward when I wanted to slip away he wouldn't let me go, and I had a glass of wine with him and the organizers, and then I drove him to the station, even though he could perfectly well have walked. In the station car park we kissed for so long that he almost missed his train. Strange as it may sound, it was much more intimate than sex in the woods with him. After that, I was gone on him.

That's a line that sounds like it might have come out of a YA novel. After that, I was gone on him. But I like it just the same. Why shouldn't she say that if she feels like it? I don't think I've ever been gone on anyone.

And that was just the beginning, says Judith. Beginnings are all well and good, but they matter less than you might think. What matters is what comes after, the work. But she's not telling me about that.

Now I want to tell you something. In our classroom in elementary school we had a little aquarium with bright little guppies in it. Everyone took turns to feed the fish, there was a schedule on the board that told you whose turn it was. The feed they got was little brightly colored flakes in a plastic container, I can remember the savory smell of them to this day. The day after I'd fed the fish, there was one belly-up on the surface, dead. The teacher reckoned that was normal, guppies in captivity didn't have a long life expectancy, and he was sure I hadn't done anything wrong. Even so, I felt guilty. Not just because the fish had died, but even more because I couldn't care less about it. That was my first encounter with death.

Does that have anything to do with anything? Probably not. But I just thought of it, presumably because we're in a graveyard. I thought the dead fish was icky. The others took him and buried him behind the school.

JUDITH WANTS to quit her job and look for another.

Do you remember how I told you in Paris about losing my faith? It didn't come back, and in fact it feels more like a liberation to me. The world I'm living in now feels colder, but the air is clearer, and I feel much more grown-up. To think that I had to be almost sixty for that to happen! I'm sure I could go on being a minister somewhere, but I would feel like a fraud. And I don't want that.

She's going to look for something in welfare, she's done a lot of work in the community with kids and with old people, she'll be good at that, she likes that.

She will move to the city, rent a small apartment, buy some furniture and a bicycle. Ann and Ella will live with their father for the time being, they'll be gone soon enough anyway.

Do you feel like an adventure?

I wouldn't rule anything out, she says, laughing. In my whole life, I've only slept with four men, I think I'm owed a few. Or I'll change sides. What do they say: I'm open to suggestions. But I'm not about to go looking. I'm going to go to the theater, to concerts, to readings, maybe I'll join a reading group. And in the event that one of Richard's books comes up, I'll just listen to what the others say, and I'll think, what do you know.

Why am I so envious of this life she describes to me so glowingly? Mine is much the same, except that I'm not about to join any reading group. Maybe I'm envious of her enthusiasm, her joy in her new-gained freedom. She's never lived on her own before, she moved from home into student housing, then she spent more than thirty years with a husband. Now she's free, but after a while freedom can be quite demanding.

And when she retires in a few years? Then she'll draw her pension and be alone. Isn't she afraid of that at all?

Sure I am. Of course.

AN IDYLL of sorts: we're both home, Judith is sitting on the sofa, with her legs curled up, reading a book. She's wearing a short skirt, thick stockings and slippers. If I squint my eyes, I can imagine we're still students, living together in a shared house. We're besties, tell each other everything, cuddling and whispering.

I'm sitting at my desk, writing emails, and in between times watching the odd video, with headphones on, so as not to disturb Judith. It's foggy outside, and night is drawing in. I've lit some candles, the only thing missing is some soft jazz, and the scene would be perfect. What if Judith just stayed? She's almost twenty years older than me, but so what. I think we would get along. I can see us as a couple, nothing sexual, just for the companionship. I would brush her hair, she would rub my back, hold me tight, listen when I talked about trouble in the office. We could look the other in the eye and be fond of one another in an elementary way.

YouTube has gone easy on the serial killers with me, maybe I've seen them all, instead it's offering me polygamous sect leaders, again, not really my scene. A fellow in Utah with seventy-nine sister-wives, currently behind bars because a few of them were underage. Another guy who has five wives and is drawing the line there. When I'm done with the polygamists—there's not so many of them as there are serial killers—next up will be the Jesuses, first one from Siberia, then one in Brazil, and finally an Australian with shades and a psychedelic T-shirt. At least the Jesus in Petropavlovka wears long white robes, while the Australian guy is driving a minivan around Australia with a bored-looking Mary Magdalene in the back, raving about thirteen dimensions and mathematical proofs for his existence. Does he believe in dinosaurs? Sure, he's seen 'em. Does every madman, every kooky sect get their own film these days? All this crap, this waste of time, why don't I just read a book for a change, like Judith?

Alternatively, the two of us could start a sect, with Wechsler as our Savior, we would offer interpretations of his novels and comb them for spiritual messages, spread his word and build a church to him, an altar with his image and flowers and incense. Didn't he say sacrifice was required? But I would never kill a chicken for him.

This morning Judith asked me what I wanted for supper, what was my favorite dish. I didn't know what to say. Isn't that something only children have, a favorite dish? I couldn't think of anything, I have no idea when someone last asked me what my favorite dish was, let alone cooked it for me. How sad is that? Schnitzel sandwich? Chicken nuggets? Spaghetti and tomato sauce? Or something more sophisticated—osso buco, roast veal? No idea. I eat everything except tongue. I almost felt a bit ashamed in front of Judith. Her daughters will have their favorite dishes, Nutella pancakes, or wonton or pommes frites, things kids like. But they aren't kids anymore. So maybe sushi or a poke bowl or something hip. When I got home, there was a shopping bag full of good things waiting for me.

My hard drive is full, so I have to clear some space, deleting films I've downloaded that I'll never watch, emptying the bin. I still have all the proxy data for the Wechsler film on the hard drive, I can wipe those now. The rough cut is safe with the producer, and maybe Tom has a copy as well. It'll never make a film now anyway.

I take a look at the footage, Wechsler walking in Paris, drinking coffee. He gives me a smile. If you knew how little time you have left. Then I start deleting each file one by one, it's as laborious as saving them. I enjoy the repetitive labor, the little dialogue with the computer as I empty the bin: Do you really want to destroy these eleven files? I think briefly before saying: Yes, I do. Get rid of them.

Judith has put her book down and says she's going to start cooking. She's bustling about in the kitchen now. She's turned on the radio for company, listening to the news. We would cook together, take it in turns to help, sometimes one would stroke the other's arm, pour her a glass of white wine, lay a hand on her hip as we're peering down into the saucepans. I think this needs more salt.

Just ask if you can't find something, I call out. I'm not sure if she heard.

Gigabyte after gigabyte disappears into the bin. Yes, I do. There's one clip I get stuck on, Tom must have shot it while I was gone. It's from the afternoon of our last shooting day in Paris, a few hours after the calamity in the café when Wechsler walked off. I try to remember what happened afterward. We had spoken to him briefly, Tom apologized, Wechsler calmed down, said he was tired, and the filming was taking more out of him than he'd anticipated. I could see he was just making excuses. We said goodbye and went back to the hotel to drop our gear and freshen up. After that I took off on my own to do some shopping, a benefit of being in Paris. Tom said he might go for a walk. We agreed to meet up in the restaurant we'd gone to the previous day.

I went back to the Café Les Mouettes, where Tom and Wechsler had had their falling out. There was a department store near there that Wechsler claimed had the best delicatessen section in the whole of Paris. What else am I in the market for anyway? I barely use cosmetics, I have enough clothes, lingerie? Bah! So it would have to be delicatessen.

But instead of going into the store, I headed, not really knowing why, down the narrow passageway that Wechsler had pointed out and that ended up in a small courtyard, where a flight of steps led up to the Chapelle de l'Epiphanie des Missions Etrangères. Inside, synthesizer music, Jean-Michel Jarre, Vangelis, something of that kind, was playing. There'd been a time I was really crazy about that music, especially Vangelis's *Antarctica*, which sounded as bleak as the scene at the South Pole. A couple of men were just setting up a sound system, with speakers and microphones and a keyboard, maybe there was going to be a live event tonight or tomorrow, perhaps a service with live music or whatever foreign missions like to do. I sat down on one of the benches and watched them hooking up the equipment.

There were pictures on the walls illustrating the Stations of the Cross. They made Jesus look like a campesino, in the early scenes he was wearing a white suit, I had never seen Jesus in pants before, it seemed vaguely disrespectful. The Roman soldiers who were tormenting him looked like Inca warriors or Aztecs or Mayas, I can never tell those apart.

From time to time, people came in and said hello to me, as though they had been expecting me and had come purely on my account. I had picked up a booklet going in, *How to Become a Missionary*, and was flicking through it. There were several accounts by serious young men, with equally serious beards, telling you their life story. Two women were also included, an Indian nun and a French trainee. I understood roughly half of what I read, but they all had heard the call and were devoted to their tasks and found help and succor in prayer. All of them looked nice and a little boring, Joseph, Paul, Gabriel, François, Sister Stella, and Marie de Lorgeril. One painting: *The Departure of the Missionaries*, from the nineteenth century, must have been set in this very chapel. They all wear black robes and look effeminate, gentle, patient, devout, anything other than prepared for the adventures and hardships lying in wait for them. One of them is just being hugged and kissed by an old man with a beard, another is having the hem of his garment kissed by a child.

We are standing there in the chapel, the new missionaries, about to set forth into the world. The organ is playing a hymn composed especially for the occasion by Charles Gounod, and the bishop, our seminarians, our friends and family members, the members of the community, are all kissing our feet. How welcome are the heralds of joy, the bringers of good news!

Then the long journey, long weeks at sea, storms toss the ship, we sing and pray. O God, we hail Thee, Lord, we praise Thy strength. We reach Madagascar, disembark, are put up in a cloister. The sisters who have been here longer look tired and frazzled. They tell me what to do, introduce me to the work, and I go my way. I do good, offer help, tend the sick, distribute food and medicine. I free myself of all my sins, of vanity and selfishness, make myself empty to receive God and my mission. Many of us will never go home, we will die overseas of illnesses, we will be killed for our faith, unlucky martyrs of our glad tidings.

I am standing with George Clooney in a Malagasy marketplace, handing out Nespresso capsules to the needy—Indriya, Rosabaya, Fortissio Lungo. Women wave their hands beseechingly; children grab hold of our robes and make big eyes. George smiles at me coolly, but I have forsworn earthly joys and am not to be tempted.

George needs to move on to Timor or New Guinea, sometimes we exchange letters about our joys and satisfactions, our doubts and challenges, dark nights of the soul. Then he is plucked away by a pestilence. I grow old and wrinkly and die, unremembered, of old age in a bush hospital in the shadow of mango trees.

And what was Wechsler's mission? He told me once about a plan for a novel, the story of a reluctant saint, a young woman who sees visions and is unsure whether it is God or the Devil speaking to her, or if she is plain crazy. She resists, tries to abscond, but it's no use, she has been chosen.

And why didn't you finish it?

He laughed and raised his hands. Writing isn't about making something, but finding it. I had believed there was something concealed in that story, but I didn't manage to find it.

Perhaps it was his mission? Was it that he was looking for and failed to find? To become empty, and then fill the void with words?

It's about being present, he once said, being completely there at a certain moment, in a certain place. You can't really explain it, but when it's there, you know it, and you can be as sure of it as you ever were of anything. And yet it's nothing spectacular, it can happen at any time. Everyone knows the feeling: there's a rightness to it. Then you can astound the whole of Paris with an apple, that's all it takes. Not even any more words.

One of the men setting up the sound system sat down at the keyboard and noodled around a bit on it, then played a couple of chords that sounded like a sci-fi film. Once upon a time, in a distant galaxy.

I all but ran out of the chapel, and then I went to the store after all, to recover, where I bought a few delicacies, foie gras and Breton sardines in pretty tin cans and Colombian coffee and later on, next door, a perfume, L'Heure Bleue by Guerlain, just because I liked the sound of the name. Then I took the Métro back to the hotel and packed my bags. Tomorrow early, we're going back.

THE SCENE was shot in our hotel room, which is a bit weird, as it doesn't fit in the film. But it doesn't seem to have been improvised, and the framing looks as though some thought went into it. A medium shot. Wechsler is in a chair, a gold-gleaming pen in his hand like a magic wand, and a glass of water in front of him on a low coffee table. All-natural lighting, from the evening sun, which is slanting through the window, making dark shadows and a light spot behind the water glass. In the background there is an unmade bed, a few of my clothes spilling out of my red suitcase open on top of it. Books on the bed as well, and papers. It might have been Kubrick or something, the image looks as carefully put together as a painting. The camera must be mounted on the tripod, it doesn't move a millimeter. Wechsler isn't miked up, it's just camera sound. There's no sign of Tom. It's as though Wechsler has set up the camera himself. But who got the film rolling?

Wechsler is sitting there calmly, he seems focused, staring down in front of him, faint traffic noise is audible from outside, ebbing and flowing, later there's the occasional sound from inside the room, the click of the ballpoint that Wechsler's toying with, a drawing of breath, a sigh, a quiet rustle, perhaps the toilet flush or shower in the next room. After some time, Wechsler looks up into the camera, as though under instruction, smiles briefly, scratches his ear, appears about to speak, but ends up just taking a sip of water, and puts the glass back in exactly the same position. He slides forward on his chair, clears his throat, looks into the camera again. His expression barely changes, but even so I seem to recognize constantly changing emotions. At times he looks needy, almost helpless, and then confrontational or exasperated, and then alert, loving, attentive. His look is melancholy, do I believe that? But there's also the hint of a smile. The whole time I have the conviction that there's someone else in the room, that he's communicating with someone. He seems to collect himself, leans forward, opens his mouth to speak, but then just breathes deeply in and out, shuts his mouth, takes another sip of water. Now he appears nervous, a bit twitchy, he fiddles with the top of his ballpoint, shooting the nib in and out. He gives a barely perceptible shake of the head, looks quickly down at the floor, then at the camera, but I have the feeling he's looking at me.

If you jump, then I will jump too.

If you fall, I will fall too.

We'll meet again on the other side.

The clip is fifteen minutes and thirty-two seconds, and I've only seen the first three and a half minutes.

A clatter of dishes brings me back to the present. I take off my headphones. The radio is on in the kitchen playing some Italo-pop Judith is singing along to. "Azzurro" by Adriano Celentano.

Wechsler is still sitting there, and suddenly I've had enough of these airs and this production. Am I really going to put myself through all that? Fifteen minutes and thirty-two seconds of it. Am I supposed to feel sorry for him? Does he want his gala final appearance? Interposing himself between Judith and me? He will take only as much space in my life as I give him, I think. It sounds a bit like a self-help book, but so what, it's true. Bye-bye, baby, sorry. I shut down the player and delete the file. Yes, I do.

HURRY UP, or dinner'll get cold!

I close the laptop and go into the kitchen to help Judith bring in the plates. She's made saltimbocca with saffron risotto, with yellow-and-orange butter-glazed carrots with thyme, it looks completely professional. The table has been nicely set with candles, she's even managed to get hold of napkins—or serviettes?—from somewhere, I didn't know I had any. With my phone I take a picture of the dinner, one of the table, then I click to video and shoot Judith, sitting there smiling at me.

Say something.

What shall I say? It'll get cold.

There's an open bottle of chardonnay in the fridge, the lonely woman's drink. We're not lonely, but we lay into the chardonnay anyway.

Have you ever jumped from a ten-meter diving board?

No, not even a five-meter board, says Judith. What about you?

I shake my head. I don't even know where to find one.

That's not quite true. I looked on the Internet, and I found there were a couple of high boards nearby, but I've forgotten quite where. That was when our project was going down the tubes. I briefly thought it might change something if I jumped. Magical thinking. Nonsense, of course, and I never pursued the idea.

What was that Bible verse you cited at his funeral?

Judith thinks back for a moment. Second book of Samuel, chapter fourteen, she says after a moment. For we must needs die, and are as water spilt on the ground, which cannot be gathered up again.

Now I remember. The water that is never wasted, the eternal cycle. The blue that is never dimmed.

We talked about you, Richard and I, says Judith.

Oh! Or rather: Oh?

Nothing for you to worry about. He regretted what happened with the film. He didn't think you would throw in the towel if he didn't show. He thought the failure could be productive in some way, make a new form, a film that wouldn't just be about him, but about you, about your relationship, about life and writing and filmmaking, about people, about the whole world. You know what he's like. He had his own way of thinking, biography never interested him. Perhaps he should have discussed it with you. Or you and Richard should have made the film together. Instead, you just gave up.

I think he lost interest.

He had a high opinion of you, says Judith, not of the cameraman, if I'm being honest. She laughs. He thought he was too nice. But he saw everything of yours that he could track down.

I don't say what I think: If I'd been a man or twenty years older, he wouldn't have been quite so interested. True, he didn't proposition me, but he made it fairly clear that he liked me. He admitted it too. Is that a bad thing? It's not the worst form of encouragement. Maybe we each found something in the other. Not made, but found.

So why did Tom and I throw in the towel? It was hardly the first film we had had difficulties with. It's possible that it wasn't Richard's no-show that was decisive but the tensions between us. Earlier, difficulties had never put us off, on the contrary, they lent us wings. That was something

Richard and I talked about, failure and the importance of failing in work.

My best films were always the ones where I experienced the greatest difficulties, the ones that went off the rails early and turned into something entirely different, much better than what I had thought and planned.

This was on one of our preliminary discussions. Richard had to be in Switzerland for something and we arranged to meet, but then for some reason Tom couldn't make it. It was an icy winter day, but we went for a long walk along the lakeshore, imagining the film we were going to make. The film was never so beautiful as in those first discussions.

We're in it already, says Wechsler, this is the opening scene: We're walking along the lakeshore, talking, it's freezing. Poplars, a shipping dock, the view across the water, Tiefenbrunnen. There's something poetic about the name, even.

If this film is going to amount to anything, he's stopped and turns to me and looks me straight in the eye, then you'll have to immerse yourself in it. The more of yourself you give, the more you will discover. That's the entire secret of it.

Come, he says, and trots riskily across the busy road. On the other side, by the station, there's a newsstand. Wechsler buys a couple of lottery tickets, hands me one. We open them, they're both duds. Well, there was a chance, he says, and laughs.

We head back along the lake toward the city. Wechsler seems fascinated by the idea of failure.

We need to think through failure, he says. It's a necessary phase in the development of a piece of work. It could be a film on the impossibility of making a film. A kind of *8½* of the documentary. Fellini.

So I've heard. Does he think I'm a complete idiot?

Maybe failure is unavoidable, I say, just some fail earlier than others.

Later on: A story has been thought through to its conclusion if it's taken to its worst possible permutation. That's Dürrenmatt, I've got a couple more quotes up my sleeve. But the worst possible permutation is never predictable, it happens by chance.

What would be the worst possible permutation for our film? And what would be the worst possible permutation for Wechsler? His death?

But Wechsler's death doesn't mean anything. Wechsler didn't die because it was the logical, dramaturgically interesting thing. He was sick, and he died. Death doesn't signify anything. Reality doesn't write stories. In fiction you can't live, but you can't die either.

WHEN WAS that? When did you talk about me?

Dinner is delicious. I even eat the little sage leaves, although I don't usually like them.

It was shortly before he died, says Judith. He wanted to see the sea once more. We went to Trouville together. That was head over heels. Judith laughs again. He called me, and I said: I'll come. I just told my husband I had to go away for a couple of days, I didn't have the patience or the ingenuity to make up a story, and he accepted it, and didn't ask any questions. Perhaps he knew there was something wrong. But I didn't care. I got a sick note for work.

Richard had been through a few courses of therapy and was back in his house in Sceaux. Judith took the train to Paris, and rented a car.

Have you ever driven a car across Paris?

My first time in Paris was when we were filming. And then there was the time with you. I'll put it on my bucket list: Driving in Paris.

I wouldn't bother.

When Judith arrived, Richard was doing reasonably well, but all the therapies and drugs had taken it out of him. They drove to Trouville, Judith had booked a room in a hotel they had stayed in several times, a big, ugly building, but right by the sea and with a covered pool. There they spent four days in the room, the pool, in restaurants, even in the casino, talking about all kinds of things, including me, only not about the illness; not because Richard was suppressing it, but because the time was too precious.

The days went by as though they would go on forever, says Judith. But the end was hard. I took him back to Sceaux, helped him unpack, even did his laundry and cooked for him. We slept together in one bed for the last time, and in the morning I had to be gone. That was all Judith would tell me, and I didn't press her for more.

Have you ever taken leave of a loved one in the knowledge that you'll never see them again? In the end, I took to my heels and ran.

———

IF YOU always cook like this, you can stay as long as you like, I say, as we take our empty plates back to the kitchen and stow them in the dishwasher.

Who knows, says Judith, and looks me in the eye, which for some reason confuses me.

You mustn't take him so seriously, she says. There's always an element of performance. He never took himself entirely seriously either, he was always alternating between joie de vivre and the pathos of things passing. His books tended to emphasize the darker side, but when you were with him, it was more the bright side, don't you think?

It's true, we had a lot of fun with Richard, even though he couldn't tell jokes to save his life, or maybe just because. It seemed that filmmaking, just like everything else, was a game to him. Presumably, that's why I liked him. There was something light about him, frivolous, joyful, blue.

Maybe I'll go back to making films, I say. I have a couple of ideas. Not documentaries, stories I'd like to tell.

Judith puts her arm around my shoulder and says: That would be nice. Richard would like that.

Or maybe I'll write my autobiography. Or a self-help book, a guide to relationships for women in their middle years. Like us. Judith rolls her eyes and laughs.

In one of my talks with Richard, we got onto what aspects of a person matter the most. He listed the cardinal virtues, piety, justice, bravery, moderation. Plato had wisdom in place of piety, he said, not a bad choice, but a surprising one. Given that wisdom is almost the exact opposite of piety. But as far as he was concerned, humor was the most important quality, serenity, or ataraxy, as it used to be called.

I don't give a shit, he said, was perhaps the most important sentence for a creative person. He smiled, you see, I'm learning. It doesn't bother me. What people think, what the reviewers write, what the market wants, what my sales figures look like. I don't give a shit. I do whatever I think is right.

You have to be able to afford such a position.

You can't afford not to have it.

I didn't tell Judith about the last recording, why should I? I regret wiping it, but presumably there wasn't much after those first few minutes that I watched. Serenity means being able to say, All right, that's enough, said Richard, to stop at the right moment. My aim is to withdraw more and more, to become quieter and calmer and eventually to be silent. My last work will be silence, a serene silence, of course. I guess we're not talking about a bestseller here, I said, and Richard laughed. No, indeed not.

I imagine some time in the recording him grinning and getting up and going over to the window. There he is, at the edge of the shot, where he always preferred to be, looking out of the window at the world outside, which always interested him more than the look in the mirror, the look in the camera lens. A siren, an ambulance goes by outside, another story. And then? And then nothing. Cut.

The video referred to in the text about the diving board is based on the short film Hopptornet *(Ten Meter Tower) (2016), by Axel Danielson and Maximilien Van Aertryck.*

ABOUT THE AUTHOR

PETER STAMM is the author of the novels *The Archive of Feelings, The Sweet Indifference of the World, To the Back of Beyond, All Days Are Night, Seven Years, On a Day Like This, Unformed Landscape*, and *Agnes*, and the short-story collections *It's Getting Dark, We're Flying*, and *In Strange Gardens and Other Stories*. His award-winning books have been translated into more than forty languages. For his entire body of work and his accomplishments in fiction, he was short-listed for the Man Booker International Prize in 2013, and in 2014 he won the prestigious Friedrich Hölderlin Prize. He lives in Switzerland.

ABOUT THE TRANSLATOR

MICHAEL HOFMANN
has translated the work of Gottfried Benn, Hans Fallada,
Franz Kafka, Joseph Roth, and many others. In 2012 he
was awarded the Thornton Wilder Prize for Translation by
the American Academy of Arts and Letters. His *One Lark,
One Horse: Poems* was published in 2019, *Where Have You
Been? Selected Essays* in 2014, and *Selected Poems* in 2009.
He lives in Florida and London.